£1.00

G000147396

The weekly short-story page in *The Irish Press*, 'New Irish Writing', valuably serves at least two purposes: to entertain a wide readership and to keep alive a literary tradition by regularly giving over, as no other Western national newspaper has wanted or been able to do, a whole page to modern literature.

If it had to happen at all, it is hardly surprising that it should have happened in Ireland, where the short story has been a flourishing form ever since the publication of James Joyce's *Dubliners* in 1914. But the little magazines which used to provide the usual outlet for such work have had their day, and the page begun in 1968 by David Marcus, Literary Editor of *The Irish Press*, is a timely and successful attempt to save and strengthen the Irish short-story tradition.

The selection of pieces in this book, prefaced by V. S. Pritchett, represents a broad spectrum of contemporary Irish writing: here are stories by internationally distinguished authors such as Terence de Vere White, William Trevor and Peter Luke alongside new writers like Adrian Kenny, Desmond Hogan, Maeve Kelly and Ita Daly, whose first stories all appeared in *The Irish Press*.

R. R. 2

L A 2

NEW IRISH WRITING
from *The Irish Press* series

Ω ——————————————————————————

EDITED BY DAVID MARCUS
Preface by V. S. Pritchett

QUARTET BOOKS LONDON

First published by Quartet Books Limited 1976
27 Goodge Street, London W1P 1FD

Copyright © 1976 by *The Irish Press* and individual contributors
Preface copyright © 1976 by V. S. Pritchett

ISBN 0 704 33101 2

Typeset by Bedford Typesetters Limited

Printed in Great Britain by litho by The Anchor Press Ltd
and bound by Wm Brendon & Son Ltd
both of Tiptree, Essex

PREFACE

For at least 150 years the short story has depended on the newspapers and other periodicals for its sustenance; since the 1930s this outlet has become disastrously smaller even in America where the periodical was for long a favourite form of reading. On the other hand, I am reliably told that there is a marked increase in the number of collections of stories published for the first time in book form and if the sales are far, far lower than those of the novel, the circulation through libraries has not declined. There is a strong body of addicts chiefly, I think, because the short story is, above all, the *memorable* form of imaginative writing: readers forget the novels they have read, the short story stays in the mind. And this is not because there is less to remember but because of the distinctive quality of the writer's voice. The story, which may run from two or three columns of newsprint to anything up to half the length of a novel, is perfectly fitted to the intense, glancing, dramatic and summary moods of contemporary life. What we look for is much in little. An hour, a day, a week, even a lifetime can be given its indwelling value. The form is strict, yet is close to the unconscious, intimate story-telling that goes on continually in daily life, and I notice that in countries outside Europe, where new cultures are forming themselves, writers have taken at once to the form.

It is one in which Irish writers have traditionally excelled. The best Irish work has stood beside the masters in Italy, France, Russia and the United States, particularly in the Twenties and Thirties of this century. One has only to think of Joyce, Liam O'Flaherty, Frank O'Connor, Sean O'Faolain, Mary Lavin and many others. I see David Marcus speaks of a decline until the Sixties, but his new volume suggests another revival. The present collection certainly brings home an interesting change of direction in the content and manner of Irish writing. What has always struck me in Irish writing is the sense of Ireland itself, its past or its imagined future, as a presence or invisible extra character in the story I am reading. In this, the Irish writer resembles the Russian who conveys the presence of Russia itself or the American, with his sense of a pervading American ethos, fable or destiny. This quality is rare in, say, Italian, German, French or English stories; indeed among the English, the sense of England as an extra character is very rarely felt – indeed Kipling is the only writer I can think of who shows signs of this feeling. I am thinking of something more than Russianness, Irishness or Englishness – we all have our national traits – but of something felt and scarcely spoken, almost visionary.

A change in this sense of a presence can be detected in the present selection of young Irish writers. The poetic or visionary Ireland begins to be replaced by a domestic scrutiny of the enormous changes in Irish attitudes and life that have occurred in the last generation, as the country has travelled out of a seemingly immovable past into the modern world. A peasant state has become urban; the attitude to a rigid religion with its roots in the 17th century, is changing. There is a freedom to deal with the realities of marriage and sex which is startling. What was essentially a social revolution has changed manners. One hears the voice of a new middle or lower middle class; new types appear – the black student, the 'urban intellectual' for example – and one sees the shock effect of an experience, common to all countries: the flooding in of foreign ex-

patriates and tourists, equipped with their bizarre senti-
mentalities and their brusque habits, but who nevertheless
force one either to harden or reconsider one's concept of
oneself.

The effect of all this upon the writers in this book is to
turn the old sense of 'presence' into something like a debate
on aspects of the inner life of the new state – an inner life
which is no longer hidden from view by the stern privacies
of the past or by the old defences of Irish fantasy and farce.
(There is comedy in this collection, but only one instance
of wild farce.) I do not suggest that these stories are crudely
setting out to expose 'problems' – they certainly do not
preach, and if there is a whiff of politics or an anxious glance
at violence, at the timidity of the classic Irish bachelor or the
equally classic shy girl, these matters are subtly and ironically
suggested. Where the writers show they are in the tradition
is in the handling of the guarded and their feeling for unease
and not letting on.

There are no romantics here, no stage Irishmen: the
present writers are observant realists with their eyes on the
quotidian. This does not mean they do not reflect or cannot
be moving. Indeed what comes out, to great advantage in
many of this wide variety of stories, is the traditional gift
for getting through to the uneasy undercurrents of Irish
life where boldness struggles with reserve. David Marcus
and *The Irish Press* have done well in giving these writers
an audience.

V. S. PRITCHETT

INTRODUCTION

Anyone with no previous knowledge of *New Irish Writing* – the source of all the stories in this anthology – might suppose it to be a 'little magazine'. The name suggests as much – and, after all, where else would one expect the 'literary' short story to be published nowadays? In fact *New Irish Writing* is the title of a page which I have been editing in *The Irish Press* – one of Ireland's leading national dailies – every Saturday since April 27th, 1968. Each week it features a short story (occasionally an extract from a forthcoming novel) with poetry filling whatever space may remain, by Irish writers. Similar pages may now and again appear in newspapers in other countries, but, so far as I have been able to ascertain, nowhere else in the Western world has a national mass-circulation newspaper ventured as a matter of policy to devote every week a page of its increasingly precious space (from which, incidentally, all advertising is barred) to the encouragement of serious creative writing, to 'literature'. How, then, did *New Irish Writing* come about?

The twentieth century has seen the rise – and the decline – of the short story; and Ireland, with acknowledged masters such as Joyce, O'Flaherty, O'Connor, and O'Faolain, was one of the three or four countries which made a unique contribution to the form. Joyce's trend-setting *Dubliners* was first published in 1914, and from then until at least the late fifties Irish short-story writers were courted and prized by the editors of the most prestigious periodicals in Britain and the U.S.A. Furthermore, during that period Ireland itself supported numerous 'little magazines' which its established writers patronized with a will and which were able to provide the essential openings for the talented newcomer.

That heady era in which throughout the English-speaking world magazines were the champions of the short story is now all but gone. For Ireland this meant that by the early sixties only its 'big names' could expect to sell their work to what worthwhile British and American periodicals still catered for the short story; and – worse still – with no native media to foster the new voices, the end of Irish paramountcy in an art-form in which they had excelled for so long was well in sight. If the rich tradition of short story writing in Ireland was to be maintained, it seemed to me essential that some fresh, imaginative outlet had to be devised. Ideally what one sought was a way of bringing short stories to as many readers as possible, as often as possible, at – to them – as little expense as possible. If, initially anyway, these stories were the work of Ireland's best-known writers, then that would surely be an inspiration to the beginner, and in due time such an outlet could be both a platform for the new Irish writer and a link between the established writer and his or her Irish public on a scale far greater than had ever previously existed. But what was the magic formula for such an outlet?

The simple, clear, even obvious answer was: a page in a national newspaper. I needed but to find one such newspaper whose editor not only cared, *really* cared, about the survival of the Irish short story, but was also willing to give his concern practical expression. I found such an editor in Tim Pat Coogan of *The Irish Press* to whom I submitted my idea. With his encouragement the *New Irish Writing* page was launched; its success was immediate and overwhelming. Within weeks it was firmly established, attracting some 300 poems and 50 stories per month, and with Ireland's best-known story writers contributing to it regularly and the new ones it discovered (about one per month) going on to achieve successes outside Ireland, it soon became a national literary institution of such prestige that the international Irish-based firm of Hennessy Brandy established annual literary awards for the best stories by new writers appearing in it.

This is perhaps not the moment to attempt an analysis of the literary and social influences the *New Irish Writing* page may have had on the contemporary Irish short story, but its revitalization of what threatened to become a dying art can point a moral. And the moral is for Britain – whose outlets for the quality short story can now be counted on the fingers of one hand. There *is* a wide public for the short story just waiting to be satisfied, not a public which will buy a literary periodical, nor one which is likely to turn a hardback collection into a best-seller, but one which, nevertheless, will read and enjoy the 'literary' short story if the packaging is contemporary and familiar. Perhaps the gradually diminishing breed of British short story writers should band together in a Society for the Survival of the Short Story (S.S.O.S.S.) so that they might bring corporate moral pressure to bear on the national newspapers, the weekend reviews, the colour supplements, to give their work and that of newcomers regular space; for these media *have* a duty – to readers as well as to writers. And there are other prestigious publications, whose whole *raison d'être* is the propagation of literature, who have not only a duty but a responsibility – periodicals such as *The Times Literary Supplement* and *Books and Bookmen*. Those who live by the word should in common conscience as well as in common sense help to keep the word alive, make sure to feed the hand they bite on. Otherwise the danger is real. In the beginning was the creator; in the end may be only the commentator.

DAVID MARCUS, January 1976

CHRISTMAS

by John McGahern

As well as a railway ticket they gave me a letter before I left the Home to work for Moran. They warned me to give the letter unopened to Moran, which was why I opened it on the train; it informed Moran that since I was a ward of state if I caused trouble or ran away he was to contact the police at once. I tore it up, since it occurred to me that I might well cause trouble or run away, resolving to say I lost it if asked, but Moran did not ask for any letter.

Moran and his wife treated me well. The food was more solid than at the Home, a roast always on Sundays, and when the weather grew hard they took me to the town and bought me wellingtons and an overcoat and a cap with flaps that came down over the ears. After the day's work when Moran had gone to the pub, I was free to sit at the fire while Mrs Moran knitted and listen to the wireless – what I enjoyed most were the plays – and Mrs Moran had told me she was knitting me a pullover for Christmas. Sometimes she asked me about life at the Home and when I'd tell her she'd sigh, 'You must be very glad to be with us instead,' and I would tell her, which was true, that I was. I mostly went to bed before Moran came from the pub as they often quarrelled then, and I considered I had no place in that part of their lives.

Moran made his living by buying cheap branches, or uncommercial timber the sawmills couldn't use, and cutting them up to sell as firewood. I delivered the timber with an old jennet Moran had bought from the tinker; the jennet showed his origins by squealing, a very human squeal, any time a fire of branches was lit and running, about the only time he did run, to stand in rigid contentment with his nostrils in the thick of the wood smoke. When Moran was in good humour it amused him greatly to light a fire specially to see the jennet's excitement at the prospect of smoke.

There was no reason this life shouldn't have gone on for long but for a stupid wish on my part which set off an even more stupid wish in Mrs Grey, and what happened has struck me ever since as usual when people look to each other for their happiness or whatever it is called. Mrs Grey was Moran's best customer. She'd come from America and built the huge house on top of Mounteagle after her son had been killed in aerial combat over Italy.

The thaw overhead in the bare branches had stopped, the evening we filled that load for Mrs Grey; there was no longer the dripping on the dead leaves, the wood clamped in the silence of white frost except for the racket some bird made in the undergrowth. Moran carefully built the last logs above the crates of the cart and I threw him the bag of hay that made the load look bigger than it was. 'Don't forget to call at Murphy's for her paraffin,' he said. 'No I'll not forget.' 'She's bound to tip you well this Christmas. We could use money for the Christmas.' He'd use it to pour drink down his gullet. 'Must be time to be moving,' I said. 'It'll be night before you're there,' he answered.

The cart rocked over the roots between the trees, cold steel of the bridle ring in the hand close to the rough black lips, steam of the breath wasting on the air to either side. We went across the paddocks to the path round the lakes, the wheels cutting two tracks on the white stiff grass, crush of the grass yielding to the iron. I had to open the wooden gate to the pass; the small shod hooves wavered between the two ridges of green inside the wheeltracks on the pass as the old body swayed to each drive of the shafts as the wheels fell from rut to rut.

The lake was frozen over, a mirror fouled by white blotches of the springs, and rose streaks from the sun impaled on the firs of Oakport across the bay.

The chainsaw started up in the wood again; he'd saw while there was light. 'No joke to make a living, a drink or two for some relief, all this ballsing. May be better if we stayed in bed, conserve our energy, eat less,' but in spite of all he said he went on buying the branches cheap from McAnnish after the boats had taken the trunks down the river to the mill.

I tied the jennet to the chapel gate and crossed to Murphy's shop.

'I want Mrs Grey's paraffin.'

The shop was full of men, they sat on the counter or on wooden fruit boxes and upturned buckets along the walls. They used to trouble me at first; I supposed it little different from going into a shop in a strange country without its language, but they learned they couldn't take a rise out of me, that was their phrase. They used to lob tomatoes in the hope of some reaction, but they left me mostly alone when they saw none was forthcoming. If I felt anything for them it was a contempt tempered by fear: and I was here, and they were there.

'You want her paraffin, do you? I know the paraffin I'd give her if I got your chance,' Joe Murphy said from the centre of the counter where he presided, and a loyal guffaw rose from around the walls.

'Her proper paraffin,' someone shouted, and it drew even more applause, and when it died a voice asked, 'Before you get off the counter, Joe, throw us an orange?' They bought chocolate and fruit as token payment for their stay. Joe stretched to the shelf and threw the orange to the man who sat on a bag of Spanish onions. As he stretched forward to catch the fruit the red string bag collapsed and he came heavily down on the onions. 'You want to bruise those onions with your dirty awkward arse. Will you pay for them now, will you?' Joe shouted as he swung his thick legs down from the counter. 'Everybody's out for their onions these days,' the man tried to defend with a nervous laugh as he fixed the string bag

11

upright and changed his seat to a more solid orange box.

'You've had your onions: now pay for them.'

'Make him pay for his onions,' they shouted.

'You must give her her paraffin first.' Joe took the tin, and went to the barrel raised on flat blocks in the corner, and turned the copper tap.

'Now give her the proper paraffin. It's Christmas time,' Joe said again as he screwed the cap tight on the tin, the limp black hair falling across the bloated face.

'Her proper paraffin,' the approving cheer followed me out of the door,

'He never moved a muscle, the little fucker. Those Homeboys are a bad piece of work,' I heard with much satisfaction as I stowed the tin of paraffin securely among the logs of the cart. Ice, over the potholes of the road, was catching the first stars. Lights of bicycles, it was a confession night, hesitantly approached out of the night. Though exposed in the full light of their lamps I was unable to recognize them as they pedalled past in dark shapes behind their lamps and this made raw the fear I'd felt but had held down in the shop. I took a stick and beat the reluctant jennet into pulling the load uphill as fast as he was able.

After I'd stacked the logs in the fuel shed I went and knocked on the back door to see where they wanted me to put the paraffin. Mrs Grey opened the door.

'It's the last load until after Christmas,' I said as I put the tin down.

'I haven't forgotten,' she smiled and held out a pound note.

'I'd rather not take it.' It was there the first mistake was made, playing for higher stakes.

'You must have something. Besides the firewood you've brought us so many messages from the village that we don't know what we'd have done without you.'

'I don't want money.'

'Then what would you like me to give you for Christmas?'

'Whatever you'd prefer to give me.' I thought *prefer* was well put for a Homeboy.

'I'll have to give it some thought then,' she said, and I led the jennet out of the yard delirious with stupid happiness.

'You got the paraffin and logs there without trouble?' Moran beamed when I came in to the smell of hot food after stabling the jennet. He'd changed into his good clothes and was finishing his meal at the head of the big table in tired contentment.

'There was no trouble,' I answered.

'You've fed and put in the jennet?'

'I gave him crushed oats.'

'I bet you Mrs Grey was pleased.'

'She seemed pleased.'

'You got something good out of it then?' He'd practically his hand out.

'No.'

'You mean to say she gave you nothing?'

'Not tonight but maybe she will before Christmas.'

'Maybe she will but she always gave a pound with the last load before,' he said suspiciously, his early contentment gone.

He took his cap and coat to go for a drink or two for some relief.

'If there's an international crisis in the next few hours you know where I'll be found,' he said to Mrs Moran as he left.

Mrs Grey came Christmas Eve with a large box. She smelled of scent and alcohol and wore a fur coat. She refused a chair saying she'd to rush, and asked me to untie the red twine and paper.

A toy airplane stood inside the box, it was painted white and blue and the tyres smelled of new rubber.

'Why don't you wind it up and see it go?'

I looked up at the idiotically smiling face, the tear-brimmed eyes.

'Wind it up for Mrs Grey,' I heard Moran's voice.

While the horrible hurt of the toy was changing to rage I was able to do nothing. Moran took the toy from my hand and wound it up. A light flashed on and off on the tail as it raced across the cement and the propellors turned.

13

'It was too much for you to bring,' Moran said in his politic voice.

'I thought it was rather nice when he refused the money. My own poor boy loved nothing better than model airplanes for Christmas.' She was again on the verge of tears.

'We all still feel for that tragedy,' Moran said and urged, 'Thank Mrs Grey for such a lovely present. It's far too good.'

'I think it's useless.' I could no longer hold back rage, and began to sob. I have only a vague memory afterwards except the voice of Moran accompanying her to the door with excuses and apologies.

'I should have known better than to trust a Homeboy,' Moran said when he came back. 'Not only did you do me out of the pound but you go and insult the woman and her dead son. You're going to make quick time back to where you came from, my tulip.'

Moran stirred the aeroplane with his boot as if he wished to kick it but dared not out of respect for the money it had cost.

'Well you'll have a good flight in it this Christmas.'

The two-hour bell went for Midnight Mass; and as Moran hurried for the pub to get drinks before Mass, Mrs Moran started to strip the windows of curtains and to set a single candle to burn in each window. Later, as we made our way to the church, candles burned in the windows of all the houses and the church was ablaze with light. I was ashamed of the small old woman as we walked up between the crowded benches to where a steward directed us to a seat in the women's side-altar. In the smell of burning wax and flowers and damp stone, I got out the brown beads and the black prayerbook with the gold cross on the cover they'd given me in the Home to prepare for the two hours of boredom Midnight Mass meant, but it did not turn out that way, it was to be a lucky Christmas. A drunken policeman, Guard Mullins, had got past the stewards on the lookout for drunks at the door and into the women's sidechapel. As Mass began he started to tell the schoolteacher's wife how much everybody knew about her downstairs while she'd worked in the bar before assuming the fur coat of respectability. The stewards had a hurried consultation whether to eject him or not and decided it'd probably cause less scandal to leave him as he was. They seemed right for he quietened into a drunken stupor until the Monsignor climbed into the pulpit to begin his annual hour of the season of peace and glad tidings. As soon as he began, 'In the name of the Father and of the Son and of the Holy Ghost. This Christmas, my dearly beloved children in Christ, I wish . . .' Mullins woke to applaud with a hearty, 'Hear, hear. I couldn't approve more. You're a man after my own heart. Down with the hypocrites!' The Monsignor looked towards the policeman and then at the stewards, but as he was greeted by another, 'Hear, hear!' he closed his notes and in a voice of acid wished everybody a holy and happy Christmas, and angrily climbed from the pulpit to conclude the shortest Midnight Mass the church had ever known. It was not, though, the end of the entertainment. As the communicants came from the rails Mullins singled out the tax collector, who walked down the aisle with eyes closed in bowed head and hands rigidly joined, to shout, 'There's the biggest hypocrite in the parish,' which delighted almost everybody.

I thought of Mullins as my friend as I went past the lighted candles in the window, and felt for the first time proud to be a ward of state. I avoided Moran and his wife and from the attic I listened with glee to them criticizing Mullins. When the voices died I came quietly down to take a box of matches and the airplane and go to the jennet's stable. I gathered dry straw in a heap and as I lit it and the smoke rose he gave his human squeal until I untied him and he was able to put his nostrils in the thick of the smoke. By the light of the burning straw I put the blue and white toy against the wall and started to kick. Each kick I gave, it seemed a new sweetness was injected into my blood. For such a pretty toy it took few kicks to reduce it to shapelessness and then in the last flames of the straw I jumped on it on the stable floor where the jennet was already nosing me to put more straw on the dying fire.

I was glad as I quietened that I'd torn up in the train the letter that I was supposed to give unopened to Moran. I

15

felt, out of the destruction of the airplane, a new life for me had already started to grow from the stupidity of human wishes. I'd never felt so happy in my life.

THE NIGHT WE RODE WITH SARSFIELD

by Benedict Kiely

That was the house where I put the gooseberries back on the bushes by sticking them on the thorns. It wasn't one house but two houses under one roof, a thatched roof. Before I remember being there, I was there.

We came from the small village of Dromore to the big town of Omagh, the county town of Tyrone, in the spring of 1920 – bad times in Ireland ('Violence upon the roads/ Violence of horses'), particularly bad times in the north-east corner of Ulster. There have been any God's amount of bad times in the north-east corner of Ulster. There were no houses going in the big town, and the nearest one my father could find to his work was three miles away in the townland of Drumragh and under the one roof with Willy and Jinny Norris, a Presbyterian couple, brother and sister. They were small farmers.

That was the place then where I put the gooseberries back on the bushes by impaling them on the thorns. But not just yet, because I wasn't twelve months old, a good age for a man and one of the best he's ever liable to experience – more care is taken of him, especially by women. No, the impaling of the gooseberries took place seven to eight years later. For, although we were only there six or so months until my father got a place in the town, we went on visiting Willy

17

and Jinny until they died, and my father walked at their funeral and entered their church and knelt with the congregation – a thing that Roman Catholics were by no means then supposed to do. Not knelt, exactly, but rested the hips on the seat and inclined the head. Ulster Presbyterians don't kneel – not even to God above.

It was a good lasting friendship with Willy and Jinny. There's an Irish proverb: *Nil aitheantas go haontigheas.* Or, You don't know anybody until you've lived in the one house with them. Not one house, though, in this case, but two houses under one roof, which may be the next-best thing.

Willy and Jinny had the one funeral because one night the house burned down – by accident. Nowadays, when you say that a house or a shop or a pub or a factory burned down, it seems necessary to add 'by accident'. Although the neighbours, living next door in our house, did their best to rescue them and to save the whole structure with buckets of water from the spring well that was down there surrounded by gooseberry bushes, they died, Willy from suffocation, Jinny from shock – the shock of the whole happening, perhaps the shock of loneliness at knowing that Willy was dead and that the long quiet evenings were over. However sadly and roughly they left the world, they went, I know, to a Heaven of carefully kept harvest fields, and Orange lilies in bloom on the lawn before the farmhouse, and trees heavy with fruit, and those long evenings spent spelling out, by the combined light of oil lamp and hearth fire, the contents of the *Christian Herald*. My three sisters, who were all older than me, said that that was the only literature, apart from the Bible, they had ever seen in the house, but, at the time, that didn't mean much to me.

The place they lived in must have been the quietest place in the world. This was the way to get there.

The Cannonhill road went up from the town in three steps, but these steps could only be taken by Titans. Halfway up the second step there was a tarred timber barn, behind which such of the young as fancied and some as didn't used to box. There, my elder brother chopped one of the town's bullies, who was a head fighter, on the soft

18

section of the crown of his head as he came charging like a bull, which cured him of head fighting for a long time. Every boy has an elder brother who can box.

The barn belonged to a farmer who would leave a team of horses standing in the field and go follow a brass band for the length of a day. Since the town had two brass bands, one military, one civilian, his sowing was always dilatory and his harvests very close to Christmas. He owned a butcher shop in the town, but he had the word 'butcher' painted out and replaced by the word 'flesher', which some joker had told him was more modern and polite but which a lot of people thought wasn't exactly decent.

If you looked back from Cannonhill, the prospect was really something: the whole town, spires and all. You could see clear down into some of the streets, along the winding river or rivers, across the valley to the red brick of the county hospital, and beyond all that to the mountains – Glenhordial, where the water came from, Gortin Gap and Mullaghcarn, and the high Sperrins. Sometime in the past, nobody knew when, there must have been a gun emplacement on Cannonhill, which gave the place its name. Some of the local learned men talked vaguely about Oliver Cromwell, but he was never near the place. There were, though, guns there in 1941, when a visit from the Germans seemed imminent, and, indeed, they came near enough to bomb Belfast and Pennyburn in Derry City and were heard in the darkness over our town. The whole population of Gallowshill, where I came from, took off for refuge up the three titanic steps of the Cannonhill road. It was a lovely June night, though, and everybody enjoyed himself.

Beyond the ridge of Cannonhill lay the heart of quietness. The road goes down in easy curves through good farmland to the Drumragh River and the old graveyard, where the gateway was closed with concrete and stone long before my time, and the dead were sealed off forever. There's a sort of stile made out of protruding stones in the high wall, and within everything is desolation – a fragment of a church wall that might be medieval, waist-high stagnant grass, table tombstones made anonymous by moss and lichen, a sinister hollow like a huge shell hole in the centre of the place where the dead, also anonymous, of the great famine of the eighteen-forties were thrown coffinless, one on top of the other. A man who went to school with me used to call that hollow the navel of nothing and to explain in gruesome detail why and how the earth that once had been mounded had sunk into a hollow.

That same man ran away from home in 1938 to join the British Navy. He survived the sinking of three destroyers on which he was a crew member: once, off the Faeroes in a ship inappropriately called the H.M.S. Khartoum; once, for a change of temperature, in the Red Sea; and a third time, at the Battle of Crete. It may be that the crew of the fourth destroyer he joined looked at him with some misgiving. A fellow-townsman who had the misfortune to be in Crete as a groundsman with the R.A.F., when the Germans were coming in low and dropping all sorts of unpleasant things, to the great danger of life and limb, found a hole in the ground where he could rest unseen, and doing no harm to anybody, until he caught the next boat to Alexandria. When he crawled into the hole, who should be there but the thrice-torpedoed sailor, reading the *Ulster Herald*. He said hello and went on reading. He was a cool one, and what I remember most about him is the infinite patience with which he helped me when, impelled by a passion for history, I decided to clean all the table tombstones in old Drumagh and recall from namelessness and oblivion the decent people who were buried there. It was a big project. Not surprisingly, it was never completed, never even properly commenced, but it brought us one discovery: that one of the four people, all priests, buried under a stone that was flat to the ground and circled by giant yews was a Mac Cathmhaoil (you could English it as Campbell) who had in history been known as the Sagart Costarnocht (the barefooted priest) because he went about without boots or socks, and who in the penal days of proscribed Catholicism had said Mass in the open air at the Mass rock on Corra Duine Mountain.

For that discovery, our own parish priest praised us from the pulpit. He was a stern Irish republican who had been to the Irish College in Rome and met D'Annunzio and approved of him, and always spoke of the Six Counties of east Ulster as Hibernia Irredenta. He was also, as became his calling, a stern Roman Catholic, and an antiquarian. In honour of the past and the shadow of the proscribed and barefooted priest, he had read the Mass one Sunday at the rock on Corra Duine and watched in glory on the summit like the Lord himself as the congregation trooped in over the mountain from seven separate parishes.

This ground is littered with things, cluttered with memories and multiple associations. It is a long three miles from Gallowshill to the house of Willy and Jinny Norris, its laneway red-sanded, like a tunnel with high hawthorn hedges and sycamores and ash trees shining white and naked. I walked those miles so often with my mother and my sisters, and later on with friends, and long after Willy and Jinny were gone and the house a blackened ruin, the lawn a wilderness, the gooseberry bushes gone to seed, the Orange lilies extinguished – miniature suns that would never rise again in that place, any more than life would ever come back to the empty mansion of Johnny Pet Wilson. That was just to the left, before you turned into the Norris laneway.

My father had known Johnny Pet and afterwards had woven mythologies about him – a big Presbyterian farmer, the meanest and oddest man that had ever lived in those parts. When his hired men, mostly Gaelic speakers from West Donegal, once asked him for jam or treacle or syrup or, God help us, butter itself, to moisten their dry bread, he said: 'Do you say your prayers?'

'Yes, Boss.'

'Do you say the Lord's Prayer?'

'Yes, Boss.'

'Well, in the Lord's Prayer it says, "Give us this day our daily bread". Damn the word about jam or treacle or syrup or butter!'

When he bought provisions in a shop in the town, he specified: So much of labouring man's bacon and so much of the good bacon. For the hired men, the imported long-bottom American bacon. For himself, the Limerick ham.

He rose between four and five in the morning and expected

his men to be already out and about. He went around with
an old potato sack on his shoulders like a shawl, and was
followed always by a giant of a gentleman goat, stepping
like a king's war-horse. The goat would attack you if you
angered Johnny Pet, and when Johnny died the goat lay
down and died on the same day. Their ghosts walked,
it was well known, in the abandoned orchard where the
apples had become half crabs, through gaps in hedges and
broken fences, and in the roofless rooms of the ruined house.
Nobody had ever wanted to live there after the goat and
Johnny Pet died. There were no relatives even to claim the
hoarded fortune.

If the goat had lived, my father said, he might have had
the money and the place.

The poor Donegals, my mother would say as she walked
past Johnny Pet's ghost, and the ghost of the goat, on the
way to see Willy and Jinny. Oh, the poor Donegals.

It was a phrase her mother had used when, from the
doorstep of the farmhouse in which my mother was reared,
the old lady would look west on a clear day and see the tip
of the white cone of Mount Errigal, the Cock o' the North,
sixty or more miles away, standing up and shining with shale
over Gweedore and the Rosses of Donegal and by the edge
of the open Atlantic. From that hard coast, a treeless place
of diminutive fields fenced by drystone walls, of rocks,
mountains, small lakes, empty moors and ocean winds, the
young Donegal people (both sexes) used to walk eastward,
sometimes barefoot, to hire out in the rich farms along the
valley of the Strule, the Mourne, and the Foyle – three fine
names for different stages of the same river.

Or the young people, some of them hardly into their
teens, might travel as far even as the potato fields of Fife-
shire or Ayrshire. They'd stand in the streets at the hiring
fairs to be eyed by the farmers, even to have their biceps
tested to see what work was in them. The last of the hiring
fairs I saw in Omagh was in the early nineteen-thirties, but
by that time everybody was well dressed and wore boots,
and the institution, God be praised, was doomed. There was
a big war on the way and the promise of work for all. But
my mother, remembering the old days and thinking perhaps

more of her own mother than of the plight of the migratory labourers, would say: 'The poor Donegals. Ah, the poor Donegals.'

Then up the sheltered, red-sanded boreen, or laneway – the Gaelic word would never at that time have been used by Ulster Presbyterians – to the glory of the Orange lilies and the trim land and, in the season, the trees heavy with fruit. The gooseberries I particularly remember because of the day when I raided the bushes more than somewhat, to the fearful extent of a black-paper fourteen-pound sugar bag packed full of them. My sisters reproved me. In a fit of remorse, I began to stick the berries back on the thorns. Later in life, I found out that plucked fruit is plucked forever and that berries do not grow on thorns.

Then another day, my sisters said: 'Sing a song for Jinny and Willy.' Some children suffer a lot when adults ask them to sing or recite. There's never really much asking about it. It's more a matter of get up and show your paces and how clever you are, like a dancing dog in a circus – either that or know the lash, or the joys of going to bed supperless. Or sometimes it's bribery: Sing up and you'll get this or that.

Once, I remember – can I ever forget it? – the reverend mother of a convent in Belfast gave me a box of chocolates because in the presence of my mother and my cousin, who was a nun, and half the community I brazenly sang:

> 'Let Erin remember the days of old
> Ere her faithless sons betrayed her,
> When Malachi wore the collar of gold
> Which he won from her proud invader.'

But that was one of the exceptionally lucky days. I often wondered, too, where the reverend mother got the box of chocolates. You didn't expect to find boxes of chocolates lying around convents in those austere days. She dived the depth of her right arm for them in a sort of trousers pocket in her habit, and the memory of them and of the way I won them ever after braced me in vigour (as the poet said) when asked to give a public performance.

'Up with you and sing,' said the eldest sister.

Outside, the sun shone. The lilies nodded and flashed like

bronze. You could hear them. On a tailor's dummy that Jinny had bought at an auction Willy's bowler hat and sash were out airing for the Orange walk on the twelfth day in honour of King William and the Battle of the Boyne. The Boyne, I knew, was a river that you crossed on the way to Dublin. And at the Boyne, in 1690, King James had fled, leaving the Irish to the mercy of the English and the Dutch, led by William of Orange. It was all a bit confusing – two foreign kings, one English, one Dutch, fighting across an Irish river for the crown of Ireland. But because of it the Orangemen put on their sashes and went walking or parading on every Twelfth of July with drums and bands and banners. Willie's sash was a lovely blue, a true blue, and the Orangemen who wore blue sashes were supposed to be tee-totallers. Summer and all as it was, the pyramid of peat was bright on the hearth and the kettle above it singing and swinging on the black crane, and Jinny's fresh scones were in three piles, one brown, one white, one spotted with currants and raisins, on the table and close to the coolness of the doorway.

'Sing up,' said the second sister. 'Give us a bar.'

'Nothing can stop him,' said the third sister, who was a cynic.

She was right. Or almost. Up I was and at it, with a song learned from another cousin, the nun's brother, who had been in the I.R.A. camp in the Sperrin Mountains in 1920:

> 'We're off to Dublin in the green and the blue,
> Our helmets glitter in the sun,
> Our baynots flash like lightning
> To the rattle of the Thompson gun.
> It's the dear old flag of Ireland, boys,
> That proudly waves on high,
> And the password of our order is:
> We'll conquer or we'll die.'

The kettle sputtered and spat and boiled over. Jinny dived for it before the water could hit the ashes and raise a stink, or scald the backs of my legs where I stood shouting treason at Willy and the dummy in the bowler and the teetotaller's blue sash. It may have been a loyal Orange kettle. Willy was weeping with laughter and wiping the back of his left hand sideways across his eyes and his red moustache. In the confusion, the eldest sister, purple in the face with embarrassment, said: 'He's much better at reciting than singing.'

So I was – and proud of it. Off I went into a thundering, galloping poem learned by heart from *Our Boys*, a magazine that was nothing if not patriotic, and was produced in Dublin by the Irish Christian Brothers:

> 'The night we rode with Sarsfield out
>   from Limerick to meet
> The wagon train that William hoped would
>   help in our defeat,
> How clearly I remember it, though now
>   my hair is white
> That clustered black and curly 'neath my
>   trooper's cap that night.'

This time there was no stopping me. Anyway, Willy wouldn't let them. He was enjoying himself. With the effrontery of one of those diabolical little children who have freak memories, even when they don't know what the words mean, I let them have the whole works – eight verses of eight lines each, right up to the big bang at Ballyneety on a Munster hillside at the high rock that is still called Sarsfield's Rock.

It is after the siege of Derry and the Battle of the Boyne and the Jacobite disaster at the slope of Aughrim on the Galway road. The victorious Williamite armies gather round the remnants of the Jacobites locked up behind the walls of Limerick. The ammunition train, guns, and wagons of ball and powder that will end the siege rumble on across the country. Then Sarsfield, with the pick of his hard-riding men, and led by the Raparee, Galloping Hogan, who knows every track and hillock and hollow and marsh and bush on the mountains of Silvermines and Keeper and Slieve Felim, rides north by night and along the western bank of the big river:

> ' 'Twas silently we left the town and
>   silently we rode,

25

> While o'er our heads the silent stars in
>   silver beauty glowed.
> And silently and stealthily well led by one
>   who knew,
> We crossed the shining Shannon at the
>   ford of Killaloe.'

On and on from one spur of the mountains to the next, then silently swooping down on the place where within a day's drag from the city's battered walls, the well-guarded wagons rest for the night. For the joke of it, the Williamite watchword is Sarsfield:

> 'The sleepy sentry on his rounds perhaps
>   was musing o'er
> His happy days of childhood on the
>   pleasant English shore,
> Perhaps was thinking of his home and
>   wishing he were there
> When springtime makes the English land
>   so wonderfully fair.
> At last our horses' hoofbeats and our
>   jingling arms he heard.
> "Halt, who goes there?" the sentry cried.
>   "Advance and give the word."
> "The word is Sarsfield," cried our chief,
>   "and stop us he who can,
> For Sarsfield is the word tonight and
>   Sarsfield is the man." '

Willy had stopped laughing, not with hostility but with excitement. This was a good story, well told. The wild riders ride with the horses' shoes back to front, so that if a hostile scouting party should come on their tracks the pursuit would be led the wrong way. The camp is captured. Below the rock a great hole is dug in the ground, the gunpowder sunk in it, the guns piled on the powder, the torch applied:

> 'We make a pile of captured guns and
>   powder bags and stores,
> Then skyward in one flaming blast the
>   great explosion roars.'

All this is long, long ago – even for the narrator in the poem. The hair is now white that once clustered black and curly beneath his trooper's cap. Sarsfield, gallant Earl of Lucan, great captain of horsemen, is long dead on the plain of Landen or Neerwinden. Willy is silent, mourning all the past. Jinny by the table waits patiently to pour the tea:

> 'For I was one of Sarsfield's men though
>   yet a boy in years,
> I rode as one of Sarsfield's men and men
>   were my compeers.
> They're dead the most of them, afar, yet
>   they were Ireland's sons
> Who saved the walls of Limerick from the
>   might of William's guns.'

No more than the sleepy sentry, my sisters never recovered from the shock. They still talk about it. As for myself, on my way home past the ghosts of Johnny Pet and the gentleman goat, I had a vague feeling that the reason the poor girls were fussing so much was that the William that Sarsfield rode to defeat must have been Willy Norris himself. That was why the poem shouldn't be recited in his house, and fair play to him. But then why had Willy laughed so much? It was all very puzzling. Happy Ulsterman that I then was, I knew as little about politics and the ancient war of Orange and Green as I knew about the way gooseberries grew.

It wasn't until after my recital that they found out about the black-paper fourteen-pounder of a sugar sack stuffed full of fruit. The manufacturers don't do sacks like that any more in this country. Not even paper like that any more. It was called crib paper, because it was used, crumpled up and worked over and indented here and bulged out there, to simulate the rock walls of the cave of Bethlehem in Christmas cribs.

I was looking for some of it in Dublin the other day for parcelling books, to be told that the only place I'd come up with it was some unlikely manufacturing town in Lancashire.

27

DESERT ISLAND

by Terence de Vere White

The Barclays bought Grangemore to house their famous collection. It was the largest mansion in that part of the country, and on this particular afternoon in June the guests were so numerous that it was impossible to get through the hall. I was standing on the lawn, wondering how our host would bear up under the strain. He must have been suffering agonies of apprehension about his precious things at the mercy of this throng.

'Funny thing about Barclay,' my companion said, as another car drew up at the door, 'he hasn't a friend in the world.'

As a caption under a drawing of the milling crowd it would have been worthy of the *New Yorker*; but it was not said for fun, nor was it malicious. The Barclays always struck me, for all the entertaining that they did, as essentially a lonely pair. They filled the house at weekends with English friends, who regarded them, I often thought, as if they were Robinson Crusoes; and when they came back and found me on the guest list again I was given the sort of attention appropriate to Man Friday.

And that exactly was the sort of role I played at Grangemore. Mrs Barclay whom, after a time, I was invited to call 'Helen', never went to any trouble to disguise the fact that in England I could hardly have expected to find myself at their board. 'You are the only Irish person we know,' she used to say; and always added 'except Michael, of course.' Michael trained their three racehorses, and he was made a very special fuss of. I had no cause of complaint. In course of time I became quite the Mayor of the Palace. There were occasions when the guests were particularly uninteresting, when Helen would say, 'You show them around.'

Faces fell at this. To begin with, not everyone wants to behave as if he were in a museum when visiting a private house, especially after dinner. And being given no choice in the matter and left to the care of another guest – and one of no importance – did nothing to sweeten the circumstances. It was usually a grim-faced group that I conducted round the reception rooms. Occasionally a guest would rebel and refuse to move. So far from annoying the hosts, this was always well received and produced an approximation to hilarity on several occasions. The Barclays, you see, were merely doing their duty. It gave them no pleasure to send parties of inspection round their premises; but they felt obliged to. It relieved their sense of guilt for being so rich. And they could think of nothing else for their guests to do. When the tours of inspection were over – having sat down to dinner at eight and with the prospect of a longish drive for anyone who had to return to Dublin – there was very little time for more than a nightcap before the party broke up. By then a fearful solemnity had set in, and parting was on all sides a blessed relief.

I could never think of the Barclays apart from their possessions; not only because I met them always in their own house, but because the subject of conversation seldom travelled far away from objects of art. And all through dinner one knew that it was only the prelude to that inevitable inspection and the enlightened comments worn out by over-use.

Among his books in the library he had built on as an extension to the mansion, Humphrey was livelier than in the house proper. This was natural enough: he had collected them himself, and he knew a great deal about bindings. Every sale catalogue came to him. He had someone to buy for him in the principal capitals. I hesitate to guess what he must have spent on his hobby, but as he got the best advice it was really a gilt-edged investment. Not that he looked on it in that way. He had the pure passion of a collector. His pale eyes lit up when he told us about a rare bible on papyrus that he had run to earth with the directors of all the great libraries in the world on his heels. The inside of the books did not interest him. It was the covers he cared for. I always picture the Barclays surrounded by copies of *Vogue* and the expensive art magazines, with the latest novel beside them. When they were alone they played patience, if he wasn't looking through book catalogues or studying *Apollo* and *The Connoisseur*.

The origin of our friendship was a lucky guess on my part. I arrived at the house with a group of earnest people whom the Barclays had permitted to visit the collection. They had greeted us wanly in the hall, then he took one group to the library and Mrs Barclay led another round the treasures in the house. My companions were not acquitting themselves very well; our guide, no doubt, described them to herself as 'very Irish'. One in particular was making a show of herself, regarding it as a point of national pride to dispute every attribution. I could have kicked her. It was bad manners, even if she had the knowledge, which she hadn't. Hers was the impregnable front of complacent ignorance; but she was not going to allow an English woman to get away with the idea that she had anything that could not be bettered in the national collections.

'That's a nice little Teniers you have,' this importunate woman said when we entered a closet off the drawing-rooms. For once she felt sure of an attribution; and pride mellowed her for the moment. I knew a little about Dutch painting, and I was sufficiently irritated by her manners throughout the afternoon to contradict. 'A Brouwer, I should have thought.'

'You are quite right,' Mrs Barclay turned to me grate-fully. 'My husband's uncle bought it from Duveen. He said at the time it was the best Brouwer outside Holland.'

My companion made a face, expressing her unconcern for a mere slip of the tongue of no more significance than

Duveen (whoever he was). The incident served a useful purpose. It shut her up; she went round doggedly and silently after that, as if she were making an inventory of national grievances.

But when we gathered in the hall to make our farewells – no refreshment was provided – Mr Barclay took me aside. 'I hear you recognized the Brouwer,' he said. 'Everyone calls it a Teniers. It's such a relief to meet anyone who appreciates our few things.'

I met them again somewhere and she came up to me at once, recalling the incident. I began to think of it as my signature tune. Soon after that I received an invitation to dine. Some of the guests were from England and were staying in the house. They had the air of knowing their hosts only slightly better than the local visitors, who did not know them at all. We had all been collected in a haphazard way; but everyone had a reason for being present – being the head of this or of that; a representative figure – I was unique in being of no significance whatever. I was surprised to find myself beside my hostess at dinner. She talked away in a flutteringly confidential manner of the troubles of transplantation, the difficulty of getting servants, the worry of leaving the precious things. In London they had a flat, and a villa in Provence. It was the devil to get servants in France, she told me. I listened sympathetically. In comparison to hers, my life seemed to be singularly free of care. One of their horses had gone lame on the eve of a race. Another had failed to justify the enormous sum they paid for it. The National Gallery in London wanted to borrow their Fra Angelico; it was difficult to refuse; but the wall would look sad without it. A restorer was coming from Italy to deal with the flaking paint in the Tintoretto. This meant that they would have to retrench this year in some of their expenses. And Humphrey had his eye on a Chaucer.

I made appropriately sympathetic noises. It was the only demand the conversation made on me. 'You work in Dublin?' was the extent of her curiosity about my – admittedly – not very eventful life. I assumed they were childless. There seemed in all their apartments no room for one. What would a child do in such a house? But I was wrong.

'It's such a bore that Julia doesn't hunt – she lost her nerve – and there is literally nothing else to do here in the winter,' she said, adding 'Julia is our daughter.'

'Could you not stay here in the summer and spend the winter in London?'

'We don't like leaving the collection for so long. We always spend Easter in France and Christmas in London, but except to fly over when we have dentists to see and that sort of thing, we have decided that we are better off here. I love Ireland,' she added rather surprisingly. 'The people are so friendly. I mean the working-class people. But we don't seem to be able to get to know anyone else – as friends, I mean. There seems to be an unbridgeable gap. I can't quite describe it exactly. As if we spoke a different language. That is why we were so delighted to meet you.'

All I had done was to recognise the Brouwer, and it astonished me to find that it had made such an impression, and could possibly be the basis of a friendship. But it was. I found myself so frequently at the Barclays' parties that I lost count. Each was exactly like the other, and the conversation on every occasion was almost identical. At some stage or other during the evening Mrs Barclay would say to me of some acquaintance, 'He is Irish, but not what *you* would call Irish.' It was an unintended snub. I came to look forward to it, and had bets about it with myself. Sometimes there were among the guests from England people who answered to this description. One was called 'Pat', and another was a major in the Irish Guards, but certainly nobody would suspect either of any Irish connection, without being told.

The Barclays never said anything amusing; and that might explain why they built up a character as a humourist for me. If I had gained admission to their friendship by an appearance of expertise, I held my place as a court jester. It was no strain. There was no competition. Anything more recondite than a reference to the weather was greeted with a smirk from him and a peal of laughter from her. 'It's the way you put things,' she said. 'You must meet' – referring to some celebrity – 'he'd adore you.'

I acquired another function. I became a social register

for the local scene. Helen (we had come to that) rang me up at least once a week to enquire about some new acquaintance. The Barclays seemed to have no faculty themselves to determine what people were like. It was as though they had come to live in the jungle or the further reaches of Mongolia. 'They seemed nice. Tell me about them.'

At first I was flattered, and then I began to despise myself and disliked my role. I was being a social quisling. It came to an end without my having shown the courage to resign. I failed to get briefs at the bar, and took a job in a lawyer's office in Canada. I sent a card to the Barclays at Christmas but got none in return, and felt a little hurt. I didn't look them up when I came back to Ireland on annual leave; but one day I walked into Julia in Dublin. She was in black, and I hesitated to enquire for her parents. She was, as always, direct.

'Mummy died on Wednesday. I was away. It was very sudden.'

I said what one says. Julia made it easy. I only once saw her express any emotion, and so far as appearances went now, she was perfectly calm. I enquired after her father. He must be distraught, I said.

'He's all right.'

'I don't suppose he wants to see anyone at the moment.'

'I'm sure he would like to see you. He's on his own. But I'd ring up if I were you. He hates droppers-in.'

It was as encouraging as Julia could be. I decided to telephone. They had been kind to me in their way; and I had been a little sad as well as piqued to find that out of sight I was also out of mind. Perhaps I was to blame. I should have written. They got millions of Christmas cards. Mine had probably gone unnoticed.

Humphrey greeted me on the telephone as if I had never been away. 'I knew you would be upset,' he said. 'I'm all alone. Come down tonight and have a chop with me.'

Of all the evenings I had spent there I enjoyed that one most. We sat at a small table in the library. He talked away about his books. He was on the track of the Chaucer again. It was touch and go. He never mentioned Helen. I asked about Julia. Would she live with him? I was curious to know if there were any prospects of her marrying, but if there were I suppose he would not have told me.

'She won't leave London,' he said.

I hoped she was well. In spite of her grief, I thought she looked as pretty as ever when I met her, I said. I remembered that Humphrey always talked about Julia as if she were a beauty. It was somehow endearing. She was, for her mother's daughter, surprisingly plain.

'Even now,' he smiled wanly, 'I can't make out why she isn't married,' he said.

I was a very young man when the Barclays took me up, and averagely susceptible. There was only one likeness of Julia in their house, a painting done by somebody who did everybody's child that year. It hung in a little room they called their 'den', Julia at the age of six – a mass of yellow hair in a primrose dress, nursing a cat. One could just make out the suggestion of features under the hair. A clever formula; I wondered if the artist employed it when the children were pretty. But I only thought of that after I met Julia. Her absence, casual references to her doings – she moved from one exotic spot to another – and her father's way of referring to her built up an image in my mind that gave the evening she was going to appear an excitement that her parents' parties never aroused in me.

She ought to have been outstandingly pretty. Helen was like a Gainsborough, and Humphrey was so elegant that he conveyed an impression of being much better looking than in fact he was. My disappointment when I saw Julia was of the kind I experienced when I saw the Mona Lisa for the first time. In that case I had been brought up on reproductions and should have known what to expect; but Pater's prose had bitten deep, and I expected to be overcome when I saw the original. I wasn't.

I hope I didn't show my disappointment on this occasion. What made it more poignant was her marked resemblance to both the parents. She was too tall. Then, her father was tall. Her eyes were large and blue – as her mother's were – but the mother's sparkled like frost; her daughter's were frozen over. Her hair was pepper colour now and worn long. She had a trick of moving it from one side of her face to the other when she was talking as if it had some function that had gone out of order. Her clothes were very expensive, but somehow wrong. They might have been selected by her father, not for her, but for his idea of her.

I thought that he doted on his daughter; but when she was present neither of the parents took any notice of her. She had her silent place among the guests, the usual visitors from England, and the Irish contingent – the Director of this, the President of that – gallantly pretending to be friends. There was never anybody of her own age, which I guessed to be about twenty.

I was right. She had a coming-out party the next year; it was in London, and I was not invited. The Barclays kept their worlds apart. That summer they had a house-party for the Horse Show; for once it included young people. I met them on the Sunday after the week's diversions. They seemed – perhaps I was prejudiced – rather a colourless lot. They had paired off, but nobody seemed to belong to Julia. The week of dances had done nothing for her, except to make her sleepy. She yawned quite a lot.

I always found her very difficult to talk to, and although we were much more of an age, I was not enlisted for her entertainment, but remained exclusively a friend of the parents. It would have caused me chagrin had I had any romantic feelings; but I had none and preferred the status I was accorded.

In any event, the Horse Show apart, no effort seemed to be made to entertain for Julia. One assumed that her social life took place in London, where, if she met the Irish, they were, in Helen's phrase, 'Not what you would call Irish.'

One morning Helen rang me up. Julia, she explained, had been invited to a hunt ball and told to bring a partner. A suitable one had been found in London and was to have been flown in; but, at the last moment, he had failed. Would I help out? It was very short notice. She asked me to do it for her. She couldn't have been nicer about it. I had to accept, but I did not look forward to the evening. And in proof it was worse than I feared. I called for Julia and we drove thirty miles to one house where we had dinner and then twenty miles to another where the dance took place.

It might have been pleasant to assume the role of cavalier for a change, and I was prepared to play up if Julia, for her part, made the smallest effort. But she threw cold water on any charade of that description from the start. It was a bore for me, she said. It must be. She had been looking forward to Charley's coming. They had been seeing quite a lot of one another, but he had started to take someone else out – a Chinese girl – and his sudden attack of flu was a diplomatic excuse. She knew it. Most of her friends bored her, but Charley had been different. He could do things like playing the guitar. He was also a good mimic. She was sorry she couldn't attempt to imitate him. She had protested when she heard that her mother had invited me to fill the gap. It would have been much better to have called the evening off. She disliked the people we were going to dine with particularly and she hated dances at any time. After that she lapsed into silence, interrupted once when she asked if I had a cigarette about me. She had forgotten to bring her own. She was forbidden to smoke, I remembered.

We arrived at a crowded house where nobody seemed to know anyone, and dinner arrived on the table as if by a miracle. I said as much, and thought how Helen would have laughed and drawn attention to another pearl of wit. Julia made an expression of mild disgust.

'Something hot at last,' I said when the champagne arrived. A joke of Disraeli's that had proved useful on similar occasions in the past. It fell flat; so, it happened, did the wine.

After dinner a move was made towards the cars, and I found myself driving Julia and another couple who flirted in the back and ignored us.

I never danced very well, and Julia asked me why I had never learnt to at our first attempt. 'I think we had better sit down,' she said, after the second circuit. The evening dragged on. Once or twice she was claimed from me, usually by older men whom I had met with her parents. It was quite a surprise when a youth with a very red face and an obviously borrowed evening suit came up and asked awkwardly if she would dance with him. He looked like a farm-hand, and I half expected Julia to refuse; but, on the contrary, she jumped up at once. I caught a glimpse of them whirling round. Her face was flushed, her eyes were approximately gay. I lost sight of her after that until five o'clock, when I was aroused from sleep in a chair in the bar by a touch on my shoulder.

'We're going home,' Julia said.

In the car, she stared straight before her and never turned her head towards me, so that I could only catch a vague impression of her face in the windscreen. But even from that reflection I saw that she had become transformed. There was a hard brightness about her as if she was drugged.

She never stopped talking, in a low excited voice. I wondered if she had been drinking; it was hard to believe that dancing, or even flirting, with that gauche youth could have worked such a metamorphosis.

She never referred to him or to the dance or seemed to be warmed by any aftermath of pleasure. Her talk was bitter – and incessant.

She described the boredom of her life, the dullness of her parents, their selfishness. She hated antiques and paintings, ancient or modern, and silver and ivories and rare books. She hated art and she hated artists. She enjoyed the cinema; she worshipped Elvis Presley. He might be getting on, but he was still divine. She found her parents' friends intolerable. Pansies, for the most part. If she could have her way she would burn the house down and see its contents go up in smoke with a cheer.

I let her go on, except when she attacked her parents. I said they had been very good to me,

'They hate the Irish,' she said. 'They despise them. They left England because they thought it was breaking up. They don't really care for anyone very much. Humphrey prefers his bindings to anyone on earth. And Helen thinks about nothing except her appearance. She spends hours on it every day. Hours. How old do you think she is?'

I preferred not to guess.

'I'll tell you. She will be sixty next birthday. I know. They were married ten years before I arrived. I was an accident.

The worst accident they ever had except the day the butler put his foot through a Ming vase. Humphrey hit him and had to pay through the nose when he sued for assault. I got hysteria, I laughed so much. The parents sent me away for three months. Humphrey began to go grey after that. He's seventy. Did you know?'

She said 'seventy' with a venom that made me start; she must have remarked it, because she stopped abruptly, and never opened her mouth until we arrived at her house. She opened the door, yawning; the light was on in the hall.

'Do you know the way to your room?'

I said I did and found when I got upstairs that I had spoken the truth. There was a bust of Socrates on the landing and I remembered that my door was on the far side of it.

I was curious to see whether Julia's outburst and unwelcome confidences would change our relations in any way. These things, as a rule, create a secret understanding, or she might regret her loss of self-control and hate me in consequence. But I was unaware of any alteration in her manner towards me; when I came to dinner again I got the usual welcomes, the synthetically effusive ones from the parents; from Julia a nod and a stare.

Helen died as I said; and I went back to Canada. For various reasons I did not come to Ireland again for holidays, and I never heard a word about the Barclays until one day I saw in a newspaper that Humphrey was dead. His age was given as seventy-three – so Julia was right! – and the paragraph said that his collection had been left to the Irish Government. That was as it should be if Julia hated it. There would be more than enough money to keep her in comfort. And I hoped that now at last she would feel free to live as she wanted to. A vivid recollection of the strange night at the ball came back to me. The only time I had ever seen Julia look animated, when she was dancing with a farm-hand. Perhaps she had married him already, or would now, and grow fat and comfortable, surrounded by pigs, and little fat philistines of children. Free from parents and possessions at last. I wrote her a letter of sympathy, but remembering that nocturnal confidence I was not fulsome. But I said, and I wanted to say, that her father had always treated me hospitably and kindly. She sent no reply.

Ten years later in a Dublin hotel I saw a notice advertising the Barclay Museum – open to the public every afternoon except Monday. As I had nothing to do and a car was at my disposal I decided to indulge a nostalgic urge. I always regret these impulses. As Dr Johnson said, it is a melancholy form of pleasure.

Nothing had changed very much at Grangemore; but now there was a turnstile in the doorway. The house was obviously a tourist attraction; there were several buses in waiting outside; and there was a handful of people in the hall. Suddenly I regretted my visit. We should bury certain parts of the past, and this, for me, was one of them. But, having come so far – thirty miles – it was easier to go on. I paid six shillings, but refused to buy a catalogue; after all, I was practically qualified to act as a guide to the establishment.

There was a group of Americans in the hall, talking very loudly. They wanted a guide, it seemed, and I very nearly offered my services. Fortunately I held my tongue, for at that moment a party which had been touring the house debouched into the hall again.

The next conducted tour would be at four, I heard the porter say. The Americans obediently formed a queue. The guide turned away, to rest I suppose until the time came to lead the next party round. I caught a glimpse of her. 'Julia,' I cried. She stopped to see who had called her name. But as I crossed the hall she gave no sign of recognition. She had changed very little, and I would have known her anywhere. I knew I had put on weight and shed some hair, but had I become totally unrecognizable?

'Have you forgotten me?'

She remembered then. I asked her how she was. She said she was quite well. I asked her where she was living. 'Here,' she said. 'What are you doing now?' she inquired, after a pause. I was still in Canada, I explained. 'I was in Dublin for a few days and wanted to recall the pleasant times I had in this wonderful house.'

She let the remark pass, and nothing came to mind to add to it.

'If you will forgive me,' she said, 'I must bring the next lot round.'

She didn't wait for my reply, but stepped into the hall and shouted, 'This way, please.'

It didn't sound like Julia's voice, as I remembered it; but then, I had not heard it very often. Nor was it like her mother's, which had the tinkle of small glass. And this had a different kind of hardness. Then I remembered Humphrey hailing a taxi. She had her father's voice. It was something else he had left her.

A MELANCHOLY TALE OF JEALOUSY AND ITS CONSEQUENCES

by Peter Luke
In happy memory of
Desmond Williams of Tullamore

'Beagles will be beagles, my dear fellow,' observed Lord Cappoquin, knocking the stopper off a piece of Waterford with the poker. 'You can't blame them if they prefer the scent of aniseed to the stink of hare – *n'est-ce pas*, Mulcahy?'

The last named, an ape, bared his yellow canines uneasily and eased himself back in his chair.

'I thought you'd take the point, Mulcahy. You observe, Morragh,' he said, turning to a gentleman in a green hunt coat, 'that even Mulcahy is beginning to appreciate the joke. Help yourself.'

His Lordship, again using the poker, butted the decanter down the polished mahogany to Colonel Morragh. But before the colonel's hand could reach it, the ape, who seemed to have resented his master's last remark, seized the lead-blue bottle by the neck and leapt with it onto the mantelpiece.

'*Quoi donc*, Mulcahy!' exlaimed his Lordship. 'The colonel's glass is empty, *tu sais*.'

The ape peered thoughtfully into the neck of the decanter; then, lifted up his hazel eye to the chandelier.

'Come, sir, have some consideration. That's the last of the bin.'

43

The ape looked back for a moment as if considering the merit of his master's argument. He peered again into the decanter. Then, looking again at the chandelier, he bent his hams for the jump. But some sudden distraction turned his attention aft. A tuft by tuft search with his free hand proved rewarding. With thumb and forefinger he transferred the captive flea to his muscular lips and nibbled it thoughtfully for a while. Then turning towards his patron, he released his gums in a coy smile.

'There's the good, reasonable fellow,' said his Lordship, putting down the poker and reaching for the cigars. 'Give the Colonel his wine and you shall join me in a smoke.'

The ape lowered his head and seemed to think it over. Suddenly he jumped down, handed over the decanter, and seized the cheroot. Biting off the end, he took the light which Lord Cappoquin held towards him. Mulcahy returned to his chair and reclined, smoking conscientiously.

'There now, Morragh,' said his Lordship, passing the wine. 'Did you ever see such accommodating behaviour?'

'Indeed, I never did,' replied the colonel filling his glass. 'I think I'll have one of those excellent cigars myself.'

'M' dear fellow, forgive me.' As the amiable nobleman crossed the floor to offer his friend a smoke, Mulcahy froze. Then leaping onto the back of the chair he started to chatter abusively revealing teeth of surprising ferocity. Cappoquin, like the sensitive man that he was, bent down to Colonel Morragh's ear. 'You mustn't mind our friend,' he whispered. 'He has a jealous disposition and I fear he feels I'm paying you too much attention.'

His Lordship returned to his chair and the colonel, taking a spill from the mantelpiece, leant across to the fire for a light. As Colonel Morragh drew on his cheroot the ape, poised above and behind him, extinguished the flame with a well-aimed jet of urine.

'Confound you, sir,' shouted the colonel, throwing the wet cigar into the fire. His host turned to the offender. '*Quelle bêtise*, Mulcahy! For that sir, you shall not be allowed to accompany us to church tomorrow. Yes and furthermore, if the bishop asks where you are I shall feel obliged to explain the reason for your absence.'

'The dirrty baste!' Below stairs Bridie, a handsome girl of seventeen, denounced Mulcahy's latest misdemeanour.

' 'Tis a fright,' agreed her colleague, Mary.

These two spirited girls were much of the same age and physique. They differed only in that Bridie's hair was black and shone like wet sea-weed, while Mary's was a flaming bush with copper highlights and liver-coloured depths. Lord Cappoquin, who had a taste for modern literature as well as for games of chance, referred to them as the Stendhal twins. 'Which shall it be?' he used to ask on hunting days, '*La Rouge ou La Noire*?'

Cappoquin House was built in the early part of the eighteenth century by the father of Mulcahy's master, the second Lord Cappoquin, who was killed in a duel. In consequence the third baron inherited title and fortune while still in his 'teens. His mother, dying of typhus soon after the burial of her husband, left the heir with too much time on his hands and much too much money in his purse.

At first content with country life in that remote and beautiful part of Munster, young Cappoquin set out to improve the breed of his father's pack of beagles. He hunted them over his own demesne and beyond: to Bandon and Clonakilty, to Dunmanway and as far as Bantry Bay. In fact, to the end of his life, the beagles remained one of the greatest – though not the only – objects of his love.

At some period after his coming of age, however, news reached him of the 'hell fire' activities of some of his peers living in the Pale and, 'feeling his oats' as the saying went, he took carriage to Dublin. What happened to the wealthy young nobleman there remains obscure. The only thing certain was that he became involved in a scandal: some lurid but unspecified affray from which neither his money nor his position could extricate him. On the advice, therefore, of the Lord Lieutenant, who had been a friend of his father, Cappoquin left Ireland for a prolonged tour of the East.

Years passed, and when in the effluxion of time it was considered fitting for him to return, he did so bringing with him a small menagerie which included several rare primates (though *not* those in Holy Orders, as Bishop Coghlan subsequently remarked). But the beasts succumbed one by one to the climate and all died except for a new-born ape. This little creature was taken into the kitchen and there suckled by a hideous female member of the staff called Mrs. Mulcahy who, it was generally alleged, did not know the apelet from one of her own numerous and prehensile spawn.

Meanwhile Lord Cappoquin, now in middle age and bored with the exoticism of the East, returned with greater enthusiasm than ever to perfecting the blood, bone, nose and music of his pack of beagles.

Soon, the excellence of the sport he offered, together with the refinements of his cellar which had matured *in absentia*, became known to those still supporting the tedium of life in the Capital. Thereafter a raffish bunch of aristocratic and moneyed rake-hells became regular visitors to Cappoquin where his Lordship, deprived during his long exile of the company of gentlemen, was pleased to entertain them as imaginatively as possible.

At this time Mad Cap, as his friends called him, kept a large staff of menservants, hunt-servants, grooms and gardeners as well as a fluctuating population of about eighteen females to attend to the domestic chores. Owing to near famine conditions prevailing in rural Ireland at the time there was much competition locally to obtain employment at Cappoquin House and, as in all slave-labour conditions, only the fittest and best-favoured were chosen. Among these were Red Mary and Black Bridie, *La Rouge et La Noire*.

The choice of these last was not made casually. Dooley the butler, like many of his kind, had opted out of the more competitive delights of the flesh in favour of the more serene, and certainly more available pleasures of the cellar. His master, however, as befitting a Nabob, made it clear to Dooley that he expected to exercise his *droit de seigneur* at Cappoquin. Dooley made it his business to see that his Lordship's wishes were indulged.

By now Mulcahy, who shared his name with numerous foster-brothers serving in the stables or elsewhere about the demesne, had grown as near as nature's law allowed to man's estate. As the only survivor of a cherished ark he soon became the preferred favourite of his aristocratic patron and ruthlessly took advantage of it.

It was not long before Mulcahy's arrogant assumption of privilege began to annoy. The first to feel affronted were the brothers Mulcahy – with reason. In the first place they resented their name being given to their simian 'squireen'. Also, since Conn Mulcahy hankered after Bridget and his brother, Finn, secretly desired Red Mary, both men deeply hated their Lord for his easy familiarity with both the girls. But Lord Cappoquin was so far above their degree that they could only seriously contemplate hating his anthropoid 'heir', and they did so with all the venom in their repressed Celtic hearts. Nevertheless, they dared not take any overt action against their 'foster-brother' – unlike the other faction opposed to Mulcahy, the beagles themselves.

These short-legged hounds had their own reasons for hating the ape. For one thing they had long been first in their master's affections – until the day when Mulcahy, with the complacency of the victor in a palace revolution, emerged as his Lordship's favourite. Once aware of the strength of his position, Mulcahy exploited it. He became, above all, ingenious at beagle baiting.

There was a high wall on one side of the kennel yard the top of which, an easy leap from a nearby tree, gave Mulcahy a sort of quarter-deck from which he could torment the hounds with impunity. A favourite malpractice was to attach a small bit of meat to a long thread which, being thrown in among the pack, would be pounced upon and swallowed whole. With the skill of a fly-fisherman, he would then gently take in the line, withdrawing the morsel inch by inch from the beagle's stomach. As the bemused beast tried to adjust to this surprising development with a few back-jaw bites, a well-timed twitch on the line would remove the *bonne bouche* from its mouth altogether till it fell with a flop to the ground. There, with cautious interest, it would be sniffed by a dozen or more wet noses protruding from furrowed beagle brows.

At the end of each successful play Mulcahy would applaud himself triumphantly with handclaps and cartwheels accompanied by shrill ululations which drove the conventionally brought-up beagles into a frenzy.

To hounds accustomed to the upper class manners of the hunting field Mulcahy was the original Yahoo.

How was it that these riotous events were never apprehended by authority? The school bully is seldom caught and Mulcahy, having his share of monkey-cunning, was never seen on the kennel wall – that is, except by Mary and Bridie.

The only thing that united the two girls who, in competing for the favours of their seigneur had at least one reason to be jealous of each other, was their mutual loathing of Mulcahy. Once, when Dooley had left a newly decanted bottle of Madeira in the pantry for his own consumption, Mulcahy had crept in and begun to swig it. Caught in the act by Bridie, he flung the decanter at her and escaped. Dooley, coming in at this instant to see the girl who was now clutching the broken decanter to her wine-red apron, unjustly assumed her guilt and disciplined her severely.

Even worse was the experience of the red-haired Mary, who was alone one day in the maids' dormitory changing her clothes when Mulcahy swung in through the window. Whether his subsequent act was inspired by a desire to ape his master, or whether a hirsute naked red-head released in him some deep-buried race-memory will never be known. The Irish do not inform. But they remember.

These outrages were still fresh in the minds of Bridie and Mary a day or two after the events described when Colonel Morragh and others were staying at Cappoquin to hunt.

There was a dearth of hares at the time, owing to the fact that the peasantry were starving. Lord Cappoquin accordingly decided to provide sport for his guests by hunting his hounds to a 'drag'. Normally the practice was for a horseman to precede hounds across country, dragging behind him a dead cat or a bag containing aniseed. Though this method usually gave horse and hound a good run, the atavistic instincts of the sportsmen were seldom entirely satisfied. For certain human acts there are no substitutes. Thus Lord Cappoquin, an imaginative man, devised a variant which had quite a special appeal for all concerned. He hunted the girls.

At a time when the countryside was on a diet of potatoes, the staff at Cappoquin lived well on bacon and cabbage. In addition, favoured members of the staff were given a bit of horse-flesh whenever there was a surplus to kennel requirements. Since they were by nature a spirited and sporting lot and in excellent health, it was natural that the girls, thus privileged, should vie with each other to be selected as 'puss'.

There was an added incentive. In an Ireland where the population of women predominated by at least three to one, Lord Cappoquin sought to make appropriate, if not proper, adjustment. The horseman first in at the kill, therefore, was awarded the 'hare' as his 'bride' for the night.

Often enough Mad Cap, who had the advantage of knowing the country, claimed this reward for himself. Between *La Rouge et La Noire*, therefore, identically matched in pace and staying power, honours were evenly but jealously divided.

The Monday after his misconduct had caused Mulcahy to be excluded from Divine Service was a hunting day, and a warm one with promise of good scent.

Handsome in green coat with black velvet facings, Lord Cappoquin stood surrounded by his lowslung hounds who, sterns waving amiably, accepted fondling or chastisement equally with good grace. Only when an occasional skirter, ranging to cock a leg against the terrace balustrade, caught sight of Mulcahy, did a soft muzzle pucker in untypical ferocity. A growl, a crack of the whip, a yelp, a slither of crouched hind legs, and in a second the defaulter was back in the pack disinterestedly sniffing at familiar rectums or sucking up cake-crumbs off the close-cropped turf.

But to Mulcahy hunting days were gall. Fascinated yet furious, gibbering with jealousy or smiling obsequiously, he padded up and down in the safety of the terrace desperately trying to catch the attention of his Lord – his beloved master encircled by his (Mulcahy's) mortal enemies. Only as now, when the master was with his beagles, did Mulcahy feel himself to be, not the heir apparent, but the Richard

Gloucester – the Tumbledown-Dick of this little kingdom.

The sudden appearance of Finn Mulcahy with a bucket of liquid and a brush gave the ape a nasty shock. Feeling himself beset from another quarter, he at once took up an aggressive posture and bared his teeth. No less malevolent, and scarcely more human, was the expression on his foster brother's face.

'Gerraway 'oo bloody hathen, may the beagles have 'oor hoide,' Finn whispered in the undulating accent of West Cork. Going forward to touch his caubeen to his Lordship he changed his tone.

'I have the tincture ready here now, Yer Honour,' he said, holding out the bucket.

A throwaway trip on the horn brought casual business to an end and all eyes on the Master. To him Bridie and Mary now came running.

The Master was in an amiable mood.

'Which shall it be, Morragh?' he said, turning to the colonel.

'Heads the red-head, tails the other,' said the colonel. The wintry sun caught the spun gold coin in mid-air, then lost it as it fell heads up.

'Mary it is!' said his Lordship with a wink at the happy girl who now came dancing forward on her fine bare feet as she knotted up the hem of her skirt. Glowing with health and pleasure she bobbed a curtsey to the Master before presenting her freckled legs to Finn.

Torn between servility and desire, Finn Mulcahy once more touched his hat before squatting to paint his loved one's limbs with aniseed. Crouched and scowling, he could not appreciate his resemblance to the ape who bobbed and swayed in angry misery on the terrace. Smiling happily, Mary could not see the dark looks of Bridie withdrawing rejected to the perimeter of the pack. Beaming with good humour, his Lordship failed to notice Mulcahy chattering and hissing in anguish behind the balustrade.

'Good on you, Mary,' he said, slapping the happy girl as she raised her stinking knees and flashed off up wind.

When the bobbing red head was lost at last to view, Lord Cappoquin again put horn to mouth. Compressing Madeiramoistened lips to silver mouthpiece, he squeezed into the stubby horn those sweet and sour sounds which while pronouncing death for some, raise others, they say, from the dead. Before the last copper quaver had died on the air, the beagles, sterns high and noses grounded, had toppled over the gripe and, despite shortness of leg, had already emerged streaming across the field beyond.

Oblivious of each other, those left behind stayed silent listening to the quavering sounds of the hounds and the horn as they were borne in on the wind. Uniting yet dividing Bridie, Finn and the ape, was the jealous hatred that filled all three. The baritone music of the little hounds which raised most hearts to gladness, filled theirs with darkness and dreams of revenge.

Acres away Red Mary, blue-veined bosom bouncing under her blouse, trod sod and turf rejoicing as the clean mud squelched up between her toes, laughing as gorse and bramble scratched her red-haired legs. Tonight, with luck, she would sleep in Belfast linen and, exempt from Dooley's roll-call, would lie there until her master's pleasure.

Far away she heard the triple-tonguing of his horn and the music of beagles barking away. She loved them all and opened her stride to give them better sport.

For those in the hunt the day was a great one. Over grass and gripe, bog, bank, wall and callow, rufous Mary, her legs getting redder as her heart pumped faster, kept ahead of the field by female cunning and native courage. But at last, skirting the edge of a shallow lake, her feet were sucked into the sedge. And there the little dogs bowled her over and, with long wet tongues, licked the aniseed off her legs, the mud off her feet and the sweat off her freckled face. Lying there, her bosom rising and falling in the warm, brown bog-water, she heard the crack of a whip and the sweet, high strangulated cry of the huntsman. The hounds drew back and Mary looked up at the magenta face of her master smiling down at her.

Returning at the end of the day Lord Cappoquin, looking forward to an evening as gratifying as the day had been, was vexed to find that the two kennelmen, the brothers Conn and Finn Mulcahy, were not waiting at the gates to take in the pack. Assuming that they were away preparing hound food he turned the hungry beagles into their yard and made for the house. There he was further aggravated to find a fluthered Dooley, who normally kept his head until the 'gintry' had started to lose theirs, waiting footless to tell some incoherent tale. Scarcely listening, concerned only with getting off his boots, his Lordship half-heard some garbled saga of Bridie in the stables. Her clothes had been torn, it seemed. Finn had found her there in a desperate state. Somehow the ape was implicated.

' 'Twas a terrible fright, Yer Honour, what way she was when I got there and it's no more than God's truth I'm telling ye, man dear.'

His Lordship was not in the mood. Dooley's inebriated familiarity, acceptable after dinner, now irked him.

'Later, Dooley, later. Is the water hot for my bath?'

' 'Tis, 'tis, Yer Honour, if I have to look after it myself.'

'Well, look after it then, and quick about you. And listen to me, Dooley,' his Lordship shouted at the retreating back. 'Make sure the girl, Mary, has a good scrub before she comes into the house.'

'I know what you mean, I know what you mean,' the butler bellowed, cannoning into the door-post as he took his leave.

In the room in a remote part of the house where he had his private quarters, Lord Cappoquin began his bath. White in his nudity, except from the neck up where he was start-lingly red, he splashed about in his tub and did not hear the pandemonium that had broken out in the kennels. Nor at that moment would he have shown much interest if anyone had told him, because a well-scrubbed, white-skinned, brown-freckled, green-eyed, red-haired Mary in a clean blouse and skirt had just entered the room with a smile and a fresh jug of hot water.

Mary's entry at that moment was possibly disastrous. Mulcahy – the ape Mulcahy – frenzied with the day's frustrations, was executing fancy steps on top of the kennel wall. Deprived of their natural prey (because Red Mary was their friend) and defrauded of their meal (since the kennelmen were inexplicably absent), the habitual benevolence of the little beagles had left them entirely. Subjected to the taunts of the hated ape and impotent to do anything other than endure them, the short-shanked hounds were on the edge of savage hysteria.

Mulcahy, having tantalized them with a more than usual offensive performance, decided now that this was the *moment juste*. With a furtive look round which suggested both the wish and the fear that he might be observed, he prepared to deliver the final insult.

From the height of the wall Mulcahy began to urinate, hosing his baying enemies below in the manner of his jungle forefathers.

The angry little dogs, snapping impotently at the hot fluid, flicked their sodden ears and opened their mouths to bark for more.

Euphoric with success and deafened by his hostile ovation the antic ape failed to hear the approach of someone who crept from the shadows behind him. Carrying a long broom, Black Bridie's face was white with the memory of recent humiliation. From behind the kennel wall she saw the silhouette of Mulcahy intent upon his bravura performance and heard the pandemonic baying and snarling of his captive audience below.

Bridie was quick.

'Yerra, 'oo dirrty baste!' she screamed at him. Before Mulcahy could turn his head or shift his stance, she had the head of her broom under his rump and, with one vigorous shove, she launched him into eternity.

His agility deprived him of an easy death, but when at last the hounds got a proper hold of him, Mulcahy's end was bloodily sure. They failed, however, to consume the hard apish head inset with its yellow teeth. Simple, emotional, foolish hounds whose anger was so quickly slaked – they did not eat Mulcahy's head. That was their big mistake and great was the pity, for no one will enjoy the sport of their like again.

When later Lord Cappoquin saw that chewed ape head, still recognizable though its fur had been sucked this way and that, he ordered his hounds to be brought out one by one by the kennelmen – the Mulcahys – and shot each one dead with his own hand. Cappoquin shot them all – every one of them – himself.

It is well known that one savage act leads to another. Woken in the night by the smell of smoke, Colonel Morragh went to the window for air. He saw beneath him the whole length of Cappoquin House on fire. He also saw – or thought he saw – in the light of the flames two ape-like figures running off into the darkness. They carried burning sticks in their hands. The impression he had in that one *coup d'oeuil* was that the two were the brothers Mulcahy.

Colonel Morragh, it is said, threw a cloak round himself and rushed out of his room to try to find his host. The guest wing, though full of smoke, was not yet completely alight but, as he got near Mad Cap's quarters, a galloping bore of white flame rushed to meet him. Then the staircase in front of him collapsed with a roar.

He stood staring across the ravine as the flames seared his eye-lashes, the hair on his head. Then, on the far side of the well, he saw a man walk through the fire to the edge of the well. In his arms was a naked girl whose head was blazing like a gorse-bush in the drought of August. The man's mouth opened once or twice making a small black hole in the area of yellow flame, but from it no sound came. Then the floor under them caved in and they both disappeared.

Colonel Morragh threw himself out of the nearest window and fell into an arbutus tree which saved his life.

There were no other survivors apart from the two brothers Mulcahy, though a sort of sarcophagus of molten glass in the cellar preserved some human remains thought to be those of the butler, Dooley.

The ruins of Cappoquin still stand today, dank, dark and beautiful, held together by a thick pelt of ivy. Only jackdaws live there now who, at the approach of any stranger, protest their proprietary rights in a tumult of tenor caws, piling upwards into the sky, swirling round and down again in swift convolutions over the ruin – a ruin that local people, with either ignorance or intent, now attribute to later, and more troubled times.

STILL LIFE

by John McArdle

It was the autumn of the early snow that Corr noticed that Ned was failing. The snow came that year when farmers were bringing in digger-wheels to be mended and horses were being shod for the harder ground; it stayed till the farmers cursed it away and when it went they hoked the potatoes from the clotted clay it left behind. On the day of the thaw a farmer found the carcass of a sheep in a hill-hollow and he gave Ned fifty pence to bury it. He promised him a day gathering spuds but Ned said it was late in the year and went in to spend the rest of the day leaning against the forge-door while Corr worked. It was that day that Corr noticed the puce berries under Ned's eyes and the ochre right-angle of his cheek. 'You're done, Ned,' he said to himself. His own woman's face had looked the same before she died. He told Ned stories about women that evening and when the dry grass on top of the yard wall faded into the dark of the sky they went up the yard together and stood for a while in the entry.

'You're a lucky man never got married, Ned,' Corr said. 'You might have ended up like your man across the street. That's what the marrying did for him.'

They huddled against the walls of the entry, looking at the house across the street. It was back a few feet from the line of houses and stones were peeping like eyes through white-washed plaster under the upstairs windows. There was a slate poised on the gutter ready to fall in the next wind, and a smoke-wisp was probing a crack in the swollen chimney.

'That's what the marrying did for him,' Corr said again. 'I'd say it's the head.'

'Women'd put anyone mad,' Ned said with some satisfaction, and after a while they parted because they lived at opposite ends of the town.

'I'd better do something about Ned,' Corr thought on his way home, and he tussled with the problem till he went to sleep.

The farmers got their spuds dug and carted them into the town before the next snow came and some mornings when Ned was kicking the frost from the forge door someone might offer him a day gathering. If it was after eleven he went, but if the day was windy or cold he stayed at the door-post looking up the yard, rubbing himself against the inside of his overcoat or kicking the numbness from his toes on the ground. One morning Corr was straightening an iron bar on the anvil when Ned said, 'I'm fifty today,' and Corr said, 'If you had have gone to England you might only be forty,' and they rattled the marbles of their laughter against the backwalls of the town. The snow was brown on the street on Christmas Eve and in the entry Corr gave Ned ten pence and wished him a happy Christmas. Big-wigging with a farmer in the pub afterwards, Corr said he thought it would be Ned's last Christmas. 'It's the women that's wrong with him,' said Corr. 'Never having had it is going to kill him.' And the farmer said that devil the like of such a useless man ever he had working for him.

'What about your man across the street?' Corr asked.

'Laziness,' said the farmer. 'Nothing a bit of work wouldn't cure.'

'A bad buck,' said Corr, but he was thinking it wouldn't do Ned much good if he knew that. 'The way I look at it,' said Corr to the farmer after a while, 'if Ned's mind could be set easy about what he missed –' but he didn't finish what he was going to say because the farmer was turned away talking to a man who had bought him a drink.

One morning in the new year Corr was frying an egg on the sock of a plough when Ned hunched down the yard, his fox-coloured coat sanding the top of his wellingtons.

'She's cool, oho, is right, cool.'

Corr turned the egg with the tongs before he said: 'Your man across the street: they say it's creeping paralysis but you never heard of a man taking it so quick. How he walks to the door if he has it I don't know, but he was seen at six this morning standing in the door in his nightshirt.'

'At six, oho, in his nightshirt.'

'Damn that wind,' said Corr as it hammered loose zinc against the roof. 'It'll knock the place down.' And then he said, 'No, I'd say the head's goin'.'

'Terrible, terrible.'

Corr said: 'When the head goes you may look out,' but instead of laughing Ned said, 'Terrible' again, more to himself than to Corr.

'I must fix that buckin' zinc,' said Corr, and when the zinc stopped rattling he said, 'There's nearly only one thing that puts the head goin' and mebbe the two of us knows what it is,' but whatever Ned said was low and nervous and was hustled away by the wind.

'If a body could make up a story for Ned or something,' Corr said to the farmer that night in the pub. 'It's something like that he wants. I wouldn't be much good at the like of that but if someone could take him in hands he could live to seventy.'

'Devil the likes of him ever I saw,' said the farmer. 'Took him half a day to bury a sheep. And I had to pay him to the last ha'penny.'

'If you paid him anything at all you paid him to the last ha'penny,' said Corr.

When he left the pub that night Corr stayed a while looking across at the house. He thought about going down to Ned's house for a while but he could think about nothing new to tell him so he pointed himself home into the wind.

The east wind blew through the first week in January and their talk dripped through the mornings. Sometimes when a magpie landed on a gate or on the grassy wall-top Ned threw a stone at it. An odd time there was a black cloud at the bottom of the town when the postman was whistling past the entry and sometimes a car backfired in the street and that week two people changed the curtains on their back windows. Around dinner-time on those days Ned used to say he had things to do and, going up the yard, he used to stop now and again to kick the dead horns of grass that grew through the stones. It was watching him one of those days that Corr thought, 'I'll have to get a story soon.'

When Ned left, Corr used to fry his dinner on the sock of the plough and all that week a slow sun came over the dry roofs in the afternoons and hung from the cobwebs on top of the doorframe. That week, too, the dust was busy around the anvil where Corr was making harrow-pins for the spring. In the steel light around the amber glow of the fire he used to think sometimes, mostly about Ned and his problem, and he used to get angry with himself for not being able to come to grips with it. One of those nights his wife came back to him in his sleep and she was crying, and from that night on Corr worried even more about Ned. He watched the house across the street for an answer and the day the slate fell from the gutter he saw the outline of the woman between the windows of the downstairs room. She had her hands raised over her head combing her hair and, as he watched, Corr thought he saw her breasts shaking up and down with the movement of her arms. 'She has nothing on,' he thought. He felt an old tension in the middle of his stomach and a darkness crossing his mind and he wanted to close his eyes but, for Ned's sake, he watched, grasping at a drowning thought and whispering to himself a story that was addling his brain: 'She was – he ran after her or some-thing and she – she wouldn't have it and she ran – away.' She tossed her hair on her shoulders and her breasts shuddered – 'and he shouted – and she wouldn't listen – but ran away,' and he turned away and churned down the yard to worry the dead ashes of the fire with a harrow-pin.

'Any word of your man across the street?' said Ned the next morning.

'Last night at twelve he was heard roarin'. About half eleven, I think, she ran across the kitchen floor with nothing on and there was nothing else till twelve when he roared.

But he wasn't running across the floor after her when he roared and I don't know whether he was running after her at half eleven either.'

'It's an odd thing that,' said Ned.

'Do you mind ould Gillespie? He was heard roarin' too and after that he started going down the hill. The next thing for your man will be the Mental,' and he heard Ned drawing in his breath.

'I suppose she'd put him wild at night like that,' Ned said. 'Some people's unfortunate that way.'

'Now there was my woman, God be good to her, and she was never like that. Not even after the wee fella came.'

'She was a good woman all right – not like the one across the street.'

'I was often sorry about not being with her when she died and about the wee fella going to England but there was nothing I could do about it.'

'Nothin' at all,' said Ned. 'How could you do anything about that. You can't keep people from dying.'

A wing of burned paper skipped the black furrows of the rafters and the wind curled dust into Corr's eyes. He closed them and wiped the dust from their corners with the tail of his black fair-isle pullover. There were amber trapezoids rimmed with light inside his eyelids, breaking up and dissolving into the tears that were tracking the dust of his cheeks.

'You'd think I was crying for her,' he said to Ned.

'You can't keep people from dying.'

'Last night there was a dog crying and it wakened me and I thought I heard her complaining again and asking me to do something for her. I only half-slept the rest of the night.'

'You have a lot to be thankful for. It'd be worse if you were like your man across the street.'

Corr said: 'You're a lucky man, Ned.'

They talked a long time that day about the man across the street and, going up the yard that night, Corr thought Ned was walking straighter and that he wasn't sinking so deeply into his feet. If he could make him last till spring, Corr thought, he'd be won.

Corr spent only a while looking at the house across the street that evening and he went home early. Before he went to bed he warmed a big stone in the open fire, wrapped a cloth around it and left it in the wee fella's bed to keep it warm in case he ever came back. He lay on the feather mattress he bought the week he was married and, when the fire slowed, the darkness came down on him like sleep. Out of the darkness the light of a summer's day came around him and the woman across the street was younger then. He was looking at her from behind a tree-stump as she came out of the flaxhole, the water dripping from her naked body, and his throat was dry because she was twirling with arms outspread and her face up to the sun. He pressed himself closer to the stump of the tree and the rain came down on the stump and watered the hair on the leaves.

His own woman came back to him that night too, and in the darkest part of the night he awoke thinking that if Ned knew what he was trying to do for him it would be no good, and the thought prodded the rest of his sleep. Once he sat up in bed to think it out but fell asleep with his head balanced on the brass bar of the bedhead. The wind came through the wide space under the door and rustled the tail of the blanket on the floor.

There was a funeral of a widower in the town the next day and after they came from it Ned said: 'The carpenter was saying to me about the fella across the street –'

'She's a tacklin', I tell you; always was. Do you mind Hagan's flaxhole?'

'Near the road?'

'She was in it one day; one of them summers long ago and not a stitch on her. I was passing on the bicycle and she jumped out and ran after me. A terrible thing for a young fella of twenty-eight or nine to see and she was nearly a grown woman. I was lucky I got away from her without landing myself in trouble. It's because of that day and things like that that I know more about it than the carpenter.'

'I mind Hagan's flaxhole. It used to go dry in warm summers.'

'God, that wind'll tear the place down. What did you say?'

'It used to go dry in summer.'

'This must have been after a spell of rain.'

For a while Corr said nothing and went on with his work. He couldn't understand why Ned was so contrary about it;

if he wasn't going to believe him, Corr didn't see why he should be bothered about him. But that was the way with people: the more you did for them . . . Ned was screwing the hinge into the doorpost with his thumbnail and rumbling at the cold. If he'd go and work it'd keep his mind off that thing. If he had worked when he was young he'd have been able to keep a woman and he wouldn't be the way he was now. Corr was thinking that maybe Ned would be better dead and that he shouldn't be bothered about him when Ned said: 'Your woman wouldn't have been like the one across the street.'

'No,' Corr said through his teeth.

Ned shifted his weight from one foot to the other and back again before he said, 'How could you know she'd die before you came back?'

'Not at all,' said Corr, 'anyone would have done the same thing.'

They thought for a long time, Ned silent by the door looking up the yard and Corr leaning on the anvil, and then Ned said: 'If your man across the street goes to the Mental it'll be because he can't think of anything else only the woman.' He sounded a bit shaky when he said it, as if he were afraid that Corr would say he was wrong.

The night was closing in on the forge fire when Ned slopped up the yard and, by the time Corr was leaving, the frost had greyed the tar on the doorpost. He rummaged into the sooty tool-box for a bag with arm-holes in it and put it on under his overcoat before he padlocked the door. The town was busy with rusted Hillmans and the cracked concrete of the street was webbed with frost. He stood in the entry facing the smell of evening onions and looking at the house across the street. The blinds were down, but now and again he thought he saw a shadow moving behind them. He crossed the street and walked up and down a few times past the house, eyeing it under his hat, and then he crossed again and paced the shelter of the entry. He kicked a mountain sheep from the entry and after a gypsy had brought her two children down the yard to beat them Ned came along with the smell of porter on his breath.

'You were drinking, Ned.'

'You smell it off me,' said Ned, pleased, and he asked Corr if he'd seen anything on the other side of the street.

'He's done,' said Corr. 'Do you not see that the blinds are down. That's because he doesn't want people to look in at her.'

'It'd be better for you if it was creeping paralysis,' said Ned. Corr didn't know what he meant and thought it must be the drink that was talking.

'You'd better go home, Ned,' he said. 'I'm getting a lift out home in a while.'

By the time Ned left there was no one on the street. A tethered newspaper was circling a lamp-post and the wind blew chaff across the bridge of the entry. Somewhere down the street a child started to cry and Corr said, 'You'll break your buckin' father's heart some day.' The lights went out in the town, there was no movement in the house across the street and the child was still crying as Corr headed for home.

He had a headache the next day and didn't go into the forge and that night he left the house to walk the twisty roads above the town. He was looking for Hagan's flaxhole because he thought he remembered something about it and he came to a crossroads that he remembered, but he had forgotten where the roads led to. He stood at the crossroads for the rest of the night wondering which way he should go. As he reached home the next morning Ned came to see if he was all right. He halved an egg with Ned and they went into the forge together and Ned stayed with him all day. They didn't talk much, but, once, Corr started telling Ned a story and stopped in the middle of it thinking of something else. Ned didn't press him so Corr never finished it. As they were watching the house from the entry that evening they heard the radio in the pub forecasting snow. They parted about twelve but Corr only went out the road a little bit and came back and sat watching the house for an hour or so. He sat on a board that night because he was too tired to walk up and down and it was a cold night.

The weather forecast was wrong because the snow didn't come but it blew its breath on Corr as he sat there the next few nights. He got a touch of 'flu but put it over him on his feet. But it made him moodier and when Ned used to bring up about the time Corr's wife died he'd say, 'I don't know why you can't think of something else to talk about.' When Ash Wednesday came he got his ashes and went off fries for Lent so that God would send him some answer to Ned's problem but the only sign God sent was a plucking of snow which feathered his hat as he sat on the board that night. He took it to mean that God was against the whole thing and that Ned mightn't last out the winter. Instead of giving in to God he stopped going down to the forge and, all day and most of the night, he watched for the rustle of blinds or the flickering of a shadow until one night the door opened and she came out, hurried down the street and knocked on the door of the post-office.

He hurried into the entry so that she wouldn't see him and angled himself so that with one eye he could see her waiting for the door to be answered. She knocked again and somebody came out, there was a whisper at the door and she was brought inside. In a few minutes she came out again and went back into the house. Corr went back out and rolled his coat-tails under him on the board and he caught a news-paper that was passing in the wind and put it between his back and the wall. He sat tucked like a penknife, rolling back and forth on his buttocks. His feet became numb and his legs began to sleep. He tapped his feet on the ground and screwed his arms into their opposite sleeves like a muffler but he had to take them out again to rub his ears back to feeling. He felt like going home to bed but thought he would be letting Ned down if he did, so he walked up and down till he got tired and had to sit down again. There was a pain gathering in his kidneys and a shiver was tightening his neck but he knew something was going to happen and he fought with sleep till the sound of the ambulance wakened him.

The driver and the nurse took the stretcher from the back of the ambulance and went up the path to the door. It opened as they came to it and they went inside. Lights were switched on in all the windows and the whole street in front of the house lit up. Corr lifted his board and threw it down the entry, plunged across the street, and stood beside the window of the house. He could hear nothing except people murmuring something low like prayers, whispering, and he was frightened because he knew they were whispering about him. He edged slowly along the wall to the door and he heard, 'He might be all right.' Terrified, he ran across the street and, as he did, the whispers rose to prayers and the prayers raced like guilt across the street after him so that, when he reached the entry, he knelt down whimpering, while his wife lay dead on the bed and the neighbours shouted the rosary into his ear and over the prayers his son was shouting, 'You left her, you left her to die and that's what I'll do with you,' and Corr started to say, Father, if it be possible –' but he couldn't speak because his wife was asking him to stay with her because she didn't think she'd last the night and Ned was telling him that he shouldn't worry and as the coffin was going out the door with grey people following it, the door on the other side of the street opened and the procession slowly came out the door: the gaunt man carried on the stretcher, his hair gone white in the last couple of years, a grey blanket over him and he was looking upwards to the window of his bedroom and into the dark eyes of the blind houses. The woman followed with a case, as straight as a rush on a calm day. She bent over the stretcher and kissed him and he raised his arms to her neck and squeezed it and Corr was at Ned's wake telling everybody he could have saved him if he had been able to make up the right things but that Ned always said you couldn't keep people from dying. The engine of the hearse started and it moved off and Corr was powerless to follow it so he prostrated himself on the cold ground till the whimpering stopped and his teeth were chattering from the cold. 'Are you all right?' she said beside him.

He lifted himself slowly to his knees and shook away the slime which anchored his mouth to the ground.

'I thought I saw someone in the entry and came over to see.'

She was standing between him and the light so he could see only the white braid of her dressing-gown and the streaky light in the bun on top of her head. She bent a little and moved sideways to the light and her half-face looked at him, an arrow probing the hollow around the eye.

'You're the blacksmith down the yard, aren't you?'

Corr let his buttocks back on his heels and tried to say something but only a sigh came.

'I should know you,' she said, 'but I don't go out much.'

Corr rubbed the side of his chin because there was something slimy on it.

'I'll get you a cup of tea to warm you,' she said.

'No, I'm going home.'

He wanted to get up but was ashamed of her seeing him pulling himself to his feet. She must have known, because she turned away. He clawed himself up the wall, stood with his back against it and checked with his hand that his fly wasn't open. She waited for his breathing to quieten before she said. 'Would you prefer me to go away?'

Corr grunted and pointed to his hat upside-down on the ground. She lifted it and handed it to him and he let it hang in his hand in front of his crotch. She paused a minute, looking at the open door of the house.

'Did you see my husband going?' Her shoulders sank a little and Corr thought she shivered but then she drew up her shoulders again and straightened her head. 'They wouldn't let me go with him as far as the hospital.' She turned to him and he saw tears in the corners of her eyes.

Corr twisted his hat a little and said, 'It's –' and turned his eyes to the ground.

She whispered, 'You'd better go home,' and her chin began to quiver a little and she turned away. Corr lifted the hat and put it on his head and shifted his feet on the ground.

'I was working too hard lately,' he said.

He watched her shadow crossing the street and he remembered a time before he was married when his own woman was walking in front of him into the light of a dancehall. Her body was held straight and tight, her head bent to the ground, and no silhouette of her body came through the folds around her legs. She looked across the street at him again before she closed the door and he struggled home and went to sleep.

'Any word of your man?' Ned asked the next day when Corr came in to the forge.

'Nothing good,' said Corr. 'He went off last night in the middle of the night. Three men marched him out with his

hands tied behind his back and him roarin' and screamin'
and kickin' that you'd think he'd waken the town and she
came after him screamin' and sayin' that she'd be glad to be
rid of him. I told you she was a tacklin' and that's no name
for her if you saw her last night.'

'So it's the Mental,' said Ned, sucking in his breath.

'The Mental surely. The people will likely say it's creeping
paralysis because they're afraid of getting it themselves but
it's funny if you can kick and shout like that.'

'So begod he's away,' said Ned.

'A cold bed she must have had last night. She's wide
open for either of us now.'

'But me and you'd watch it,' said Ned.

'We'd be far too cute for that,' said Corr, and he started
to laugh.

Ned thought for a while and said, a little unsurely,
'You're not taking it as badly as I thought. I'm glad you're
not.'

Corr looked at him, trying to make out what he meant but
he couldn't, and he couldn't think what he should answer,
so he just laughed. Ned started to laugh too and, not to be
outdone, Corr laughed louder. Neither of them wanted to
be the first to stop so their laughter grew louder and louder,
chopping over the lazy morning town with heavy-wived
husbands standing in shops looking out at the weather. It
might have been their laughter that acted as a summons for
the buck goat that came in from the hills that morning – a
buff-coloured one that dragged its hair-pods down the
street of the town. He stopped to chew the beard of grass
that had started to grow in the horse-manure at the entry
and when Corr and Ned chased him he crossed the street to
look into the earth-patch in front of the house with its white
grass nailed down by dead dahlia stalks and a fawn fungus
sucking the stones of the rockery. He sniffed at it and
nudged himself down the footpath, chewing the grass along
the edges, moving slower than the brown papers and, on
his way into the graveyard he stopped to look in the door of
the chapel where the eleven Mass was just ending and the
women of the town were praying for a milder spring.

AIMEZ-VOUS COLETTE?

by Ita Daly

As I walk to school in the morning, or go
for my groceries at the week-end, or perhaps pay a visit to
the local public library, I often wonder – do I present a
figure of fun? I should I suppose: provincial school-mistress;
spinster; wrong side of forty. Certainly I must seem odd to
these pathetic rustic minds to whom any woman of my age
should be safely wed, or in a nunnery, or decently subdued
by her continuing celibacy. I teach in a convent. No ordinary
convent, mind you, for the nuns are French, and as you
might expect this gives the school a certain cachet among
our local bourgeoisie. Most of the girls are boarders – day-
girls are tolerated with an ill grace – and many of them
spring from quite illustrious lines. The leading merchant has
two daughters here; the doctor and the dentist three apiece.
Even the surgeon in the County Hospital has sent his
Melissa to us.

The town in which I work and live is one of those awful
provincial Irish towns which destroys without exception
anyone of any sensitivity who must live there. It is every bit
as narrow, snobbish and anti-thought today as it was twenty
years ago. It is the sort of town which depraved Northerners
– Swedes, Dutch and the like – are captivated by. They
always assure us, on departing, that our unique attitude

67

towards life and our marvellous traditions must be preserved, at all costs, against encroaching materialism.

As you may have guessed, I do not like this town: neither, however, does it make me unhappy. Unhappiness, I am beginning to realize, is a condition of the young. I realize it more as I spend a whole day – sometimes as much as a week – without being actively unhappy myself. Even those mediocrities who surround me do not upset me excessively any more. At most I occasionally feel something a little sharper than irritation at their absurd attempts at liberalism. Such as collections and fasts outside Church doors for the Biafrans, when every mother within twenty miles would lock up her daughter if a black man came to town. And would be encouraged by their priests to do so.

But on the whole, as I said, I live life with a modicum of enjoyment. I have a small house, and a cat. I grow vegetables and flowers and I buy beautiful and expensive clothes in Dublin and London. I cook well, and I enjoy a glass of wine with my meals. I have no friends, but I do not feel the need of them. When I leave the victim daughters of the bourgeoisie behind, having duly carried out my daily efforts at subversion with the help of Keats and Thomas, I return to my little house and close my door on the outside world. Then I read. As Miss Slattery in the Public Library says, I am a terrible reader. I prefer the French to the English novel, and with the best, the most sophisticated and subtle minds for company, why should I care about an Ireland that continues to rot in obscurantism and neurosis?

I particularly like the novels of Colette. I have always been drawn to her work. She creates an ambience which I have never found elsewhere, except in poetry. Indeed I often think that if it were not for Colette, I should have left this wretched place years ago. But her books are so peopled with village school-mistresses, leading romantic and smouldering lives in some distant town, I may foolishly have thought that something similar might happen to me, here in *my* distant Irish town. But Irish towns are not French towns. Or perhaps the whole point is that they are: if I were living deep in the Midi, teaching the daughters of the local bourgeoisie at the local Lycée, I would perhaps find myself surrounded by just such nonsense and stupidity as I do here. It is, after all, the romantic vision of Madame Colette which transforms and enhances.

I have often thought of writing myself. I am sure I could, for I consider myself to be intelligent and perceptive enough and my retired life is ideally suited to such an occupation. I have hours of undisturbed solitude, all the bodily comforts that I need, and a job which if dull is not overtaxing – and yet I have never written. Not a line, not even an elegy for Sitwell, my previous dear cat, when he died last Spring aged twelve years.

Of course, really, I know perfectly well why I do not write; why I will never write. I have nothing to write about. Now I appreciate that this may seem a lame excuse to many; a writer they will say, a real writer, can write about anything. Look at Jane Austen. Jane Austen, I notice, is always cited in this context, why I don't know, as she has always seemed to me an excessively sociable person with a myriad of human relationships. While, by comparison, I am a hermit. It is true that I work and live among people but my relationships with them are invariably tangential. I never exchange a word with my head-mistress, my girls, my butcher, except in the course of business. And I have lived like this for twenty years. Before that, it is true, there was the odd relationship which may appear to have had slightly more substance: a shadowy involvement with my parents, the occasional girlish exchange during my years at a gloomy and indifferent boarding school. On the whole, however, my life could be said to be arid. But, be assured, I do not use the word perjoratively. I am pleased with this aridity. Just as I like the dryness of my skin. I cannot abide clammy skin – it makes me quite ill to come into contact with. But when my hand brushes my cheek and I feel and hear the dry rasp, I experience something akin to pleasure.

In my entire life there is only one incident about which I could write. No, it was not an incident, it was an interlude – a period of joy. I could write about it with ease, for I recall it often and I remember it still with clarity though its pain is no longer as sharp.

Can you imagine me at twenty? I have always been a

plain woman, but whereas nowadays I seldom think of this, even when I look in my mirror, at twenty it was the over-riding factor in my life. At school I had never thought about my looks – I don't think any of us did. Cleverness was what counted, and anyway, nobody who spent nine months of the year in the same greasy gym-frock and washed her hair every two months could have any pretentions to prettiness. And when I left my boarding school and went, clutching my County Council scholarship, to pursue my studies at University in Dublin, my terror was so overwhelming that it blotted out every other sensation from my consciousness. As I stood for the first time in the Great Hall of the College, I literally trembled from head to foot.

Today my most outstanding character trait is probably my independence, but in those days I was like a puppy. I became a slave to anybody who threw me a kind word. Perhaps this is why I dislike dogs so much. I prefer my cats – elegant independent beasts, who stalk off, indifferent to all shows of affection. Every time I see a silly pup, wagging his tail furiously, even when he is being kicked out of the way, I am reminded of myself at twenty.

I was staying at Dominican Hall, where I lived for my four years at University. Initially I was even too shy to have tea with the others in the dining-room and I would buy a bun and an apple and eat them by myself in my bedroom. Then, after about a month, I began to venture downstairs and eventually I became accepted. People came to know my name and they'd nod to me as I crossed the Green. I was even included in the tea-time conversations. I was a good listener, and quite a subtle flatterer (though to be fair to myself, I think it was often genuine admiration on my part). I did not make a close friend, but this new-found camarad-erie was quite enough. Then, as I gained confidence, and was known even to timidly initiate a conversation myself, I began to realize that I was finding much of my companions' conversation unintelligible. It was all about boys, love affairs and dating; unknown territory to me. Just as I had never thought about my looks, so I had never thought about boys. But now I did. I even began to notice them as I sat in the lecture-halls, and it was easy to see what interested the other girls so greatly. Suddenly I was caught up in the excitement of potential romance, just like all the rest. I stopped thinking of myself as an outsider. I felt I was becoming normal.

I began to pay visits to Woolworths, to buy lipsticks and powder and even a home permanent. I could discuss such purchases with the other girls, even sometimes offer them advice on bargain hunting. I woke up every morning with a feeling of anticipation, and, instead of going straight to the library, increasingly I found myself going for coffee and a gossip.

At this stage, the question of boy-friends was largely academic as few of the girls actually had one, but we all talked about them constantly. I believed I was attractive to boys. I think I trusted in the magic properties of the make-up I used and I felt that each time I clumsily applied my morning mask I was being liberated from myself and my inadequacies. Of course I was still too shy to actually look directly at boys, but whenever I had to pass a group of them I felt sure that they were all looking at me.

Eventually it was decided (by whom I cannot now recall) that I should join some of the other girls at the Friday evening student dance. I was overwhelmed. I felt far more nervous than I had ever felt sitting for an examination. But I was determined to go, so I took myself in hand and was ready, painted and coiffured at the appointed time on the Friday.

I went to three dances before I would allow myself to admit that something was wrong. The first night, I was genuinely puzzled. As the evening wore on I couldn't understand why nobody was asking me to dance. Maybe because I didn't know the place and looked awkward as I blundered around searching for the Ladies. Maybe because these boys only danced with the regulars, the girls who came here every week, and they would have to get used to my face before they asked me. At the end of the night I had convinced myself that there was no need to worry and indeed I was looking forward to the next Friday when I would avoid so many mistakes and would surely emanate a new confidence.

But the following week it was the same story, and the week afterwards. That night when I came home I locked myself in the bathroom and stood in front of the mirror. A heavy, rather stupid-looking face stared back at me. The skin was muddy, the hair dull and limp. Even to my novice eyes the inexpertly applied make-up appeared garish and pathetic. The dress which I had chosen with such care hung in sad folds over my flat bosom. I felt myself blush – a deep blush of shame. What a spectacle I must have made of myself. What a fool I must have looked, standing there with a hopeful, grateful expression on my lumpy face, waiting to be asked to dance.

I think most people, when they look back on their youth, find, or pretend to find, these intense emotions rather amusing. It seems to me that this is just another aspect of the sentimentalization of youth which is so commonly indulged in in middle age. I know that the misery I experienced that night was far greater than anything I have experienced, or could experience, since.

I left the bathroom and I took my lipstick, my powder and my cheap perfume, made a bundle of them, and threw them over the railings into the bushes in Stephen's Green. I resumed my earlier habits, and returned to my reading in the library, where I kept my eyes firmly downcast in case by chance I should meet the pitying gaze of some of those boys whom I had so beseeched at those dances. I took my tea earlier to make sure of avoiding contact with my friends. They never appeared to miss me, and I suppose they were relieved to be rid of someone whom they had tolerated only out of kindness. How had I ever imagined that I could fit in amidst their gay and careless chatter – I, who carried around with me a smell of deprivation and humility which singled me out from these confident grocers' daughters?

I became a most serious student, and it was in this period of my life that I developed my taste for vicarious living. I did not have to totally relinquish my world of romance, for now I found it in the pages of Flaubert, and Hardy and Stendhal.

After a time I became less actively unhappy, and once I

could close my door on the world at night I knew peace. I was no longer tormented by my ugliness and ineptitude – there was nobody there to sneer at my clumsy attempts at man-catching – and my antidote against loneliness continued to give me solace as I read late into the night. But with the coming of Spring and the longer evenings, I began to feel restless. An animal stirring perhaps? I found myself gazing around the library, day-dreaming, instead of reading the books lying in front of me. It was in this manner, one day, that I first noticed Humphrey. I was toying with a pencil, idly thinking of nothing, when it rolled away from me across the table. As I retrieved it, again idly, I happened to glance at the man sitting opposite. He had been staring at me, but quickly looked away. It must have been the embarrassment with which he looked away that first aroused my interest, for after that I noticed him practically every day, and he always seemed to find a seat near mine. Sometimes I would catch him gazing at me; at other times he would be totally involved in his work.

At this period there were quite a number of African students at the University, but I think Humphrey was the blackest man I had ever seen. He was quite small, with a rather large head covered in fuzzy down, and long, curiously flat arms. He seemed very ugly to me, but I was flattered by his obvious interest in me and I had all sorts of fiercely-held liberal attitudes which must have affected my reaction towards him. I pitied him too, for I thought that anyone who could find me an object of interest must be desperate indeed.

Soon, when I found him looking at me I would look back, not quite smiling, but in a reasonably friendly manner. I took to saying 'excuse me', vaguely in his direction when I left the table. Then one day we literally bumped into each other outside the library door and both of us involuntarily said hello. After this we always exchanged greetings and then about a month later as we sat working I found a note pushed across the table towards me. It read (and I still remember the wording clearly): 'Dear Miss, would you care to break into your morning studies and refresh yourself with a cup of coffee?'

We were soon meeting regularly. As if by agreement, though neither of us ever mentioned it, we never met outside, and we never went anywhere. But every Saturday afternoon at about four o'clock, I would catch the bus to Rathmines, to Humphrey's bed-sittingroom. He lived in a large run-down house, at the top of a hill, just off the Rathmines Road. The house seemed to be let out entirely to African and Indian students, and I can still recall vividly the strong, individual aroma that filled it. It was made up of exotic cooking smells and perspiration and stale perfume. All the other students seemed to entertain their girl-friends on Saturday afternoons too, and I got to know some of them (though we never spoke) as we travelled on the bus or stood on the door-step together. Their approach was either furtive or brazen and I was sure that I was the only undergraduate among them. It made me very angry that these girls should feel that they had to act like this, and also, that these boys should have to have such girl-friends; but when I thought of myself and remembered my own ugliness I was often reminded of a favourite saying of one of the students in Dominican Hall as she prepared for the Friday night dance – 'Any port in a storm'.

Perhaps this was true for me initially, but as I got to know Humphrey I began to realize that he was a person of unusual qualities. He was very gentle – he didn't seem to have any aggression in his make-up at all. He laughed often and easily. He was a cultivated person, and whereas I was a crammer – with my peasant equation: learning equals getting on – he was a scholar.

Each Saturday when I arrived he would very formally shake hands and take my coat and make me comfortable. Then we would sit and talk, I with ease for the first time in my life, discovering too that I could be witty and interesting and that Humphrey obviously thought so. We always listened to music, and I was taught to understand something of its magic. We would sit for hours, listening to string quartets and looking out over the darkening roof-tops. During these periods I grew genuinely to like Humphrey. He seemed so lonely and yet so calm sitting there in the shadowy room. I admired his calm, and my natural kind-

74

ness and crude radicalism made me suffer what I imagined he was suffering.

Later, when it was quite dark and the light was put on and the spell broken, he would make me a chicken stew. It was of a most spicy, succulent oiliness which I have never tasted since and have never been able to capture in my own cooking. Afterwards he would kiss me and fondle me for half an hour, maybe an hour, and then I'd get up, put on my coat and catch my bus home.

Oh, they were marvellous evenings – oases of brightness in my grey, dull weeks. His kisses healed me, and if they excited him, I never knew. I was too young, too unconscious for the relationship to have been a sexual one, even in texture. And I am so glad now that I was unschooled in the sex-manuals with their crude theories of the potency of the black man. Our relationship was a relationship of love.

I had never in my life been given a present, not even by my parents who were too busy struggling to keep me at school to have been able to pay for presents. Now Humphrey gave them to me. He would suddenly present me with a flower, or a hair-band, or a book. He taught me to open myself, he told me I was pretty, and while I was with him I believed it, for I knew by the way he looked at me that *he* believed it. Most of the time in that bed-sittingroom, I was happy. I learned to forget myself and my tortured inadequacies.

I don't know how I thought it would end. I knew at the back of my mind that I would not marry Humphrey, but I never really admitted it to myself – I kept it well out of sight and continued to enjoy the present.

Then one Saturday, about three weeks after he had duly carried off a double first in History and Politics, Humphrey handed me a large white envelope as I came in the door. It was an invitation to any of Mr Ozookwe's friends to the forthcoming conferring ceremonies, and afterwards, to a cup of tea with the President of the College.

'Well,' said Humphrey, 'we'll buy you a new hat. I know exactly the kind you should wear . . .'

This was a shock – I had never thought of it. Not once. I began to feel sick. I thought of all those girls in Dominican

Hall, and all the boys who had ignored me at those Friday
night dances. I thought of me in my finery, and their comments and their sneers. So this was all I could produce.
This was where I ended up. Humphrey was no longer my
kind, gentle friend – he was a black man.

'Humphrey, no,' I said, 'you know how I hate social
occasions. I won't even go to my own conferring – if I
ever get that far.' The little joke could not disguise the
panic in my voice. 'I'll tell you what – afterwards, we
could . . .' but the expression on his face stopped me. He
looked as if he was in physical pain. But his voice was
gentle when he spoke.

'Yes, I see,' he said. 'I should have seen all along – it was
stupid of me. I am sorry for embarrassing you. I think you'd
better go now, please.'

Well, of course I changed my mind the next day. Humphrey would be going away, it was the least I could do for
him, give him this. I would miss him. I would sorrow after
him. I wrote to him but he did not reply. I called at his house,
and the second time an Indian answered the door and told
me that he had moved, left no address. I never saw him
again. He may have been killed in the Biafran War (he was
an Ibo), or he may be rich and prosperous, living somewhere in Nigeria, with several wives perhaps. I hope, do
you think, that he has forgotten me?

THE LAST CAMPAIGN

by Maeve Kelly

Martha opened the back door, blinking hurtfully at the brightness of the day. The milking machine was still humming. She felt guilty because she hadn't heard Joe groaning out of bed. Sleep never seemed to ease out the exhaustion of the previous day. All the accumulated weariness was now showing in the hollows of his face. His cheek bones, jutting eyebrows, chin, were gaunt promontories under the thatch of his hair. He could do with a hair cut, too.

She sat on the step and pulled on her wellingtons, then went to the outhouse for the buckets and layers mash. In the hen-house, the flock, grumbling and clucking to themselves, heard the sound of their breakfast being prepared and set up their morning cacophony. 'Hens,' she said to herself, flicking her eyeballs upward, 'hens are the end. Who could love hens?' She filled two buckets with the layers mash and staggered to their door, bracing herself for the attack when she entered. A few fistfuls of dry mash thrown around distracted them while she emptied the buckets in the troughs. Joe had improvised cleverly to make the feeding troughs. He had used old rusted milk churns as centrepieces and worn car tyres, cut open, encircled them. It was into the tyres she poured the dry food. The hens ate quickly, their narrow heads taking up little room in the circle. She sniffed. The deep litter smelled healthy. She filled the other troughs, detached the long hose from the wall, opened the tap and poured the water into the drinking vessels. She straightened her back and watched smiling at the feeding flock, their busy pecking a lullaby of contentment. She put some clean straw in the bottom of the bucket and began to collect the eggs.

Herself and Joe met at the tap on the wall outside. He hosed down his boots, thinking about something. 'Isn't it a beautiful day, Joe,' she said. 'You might get the last of the hay drawn in today.' 'I might,' he said, looking up at a small, dark cloud away on the horizon and checking the direction of the wind. 'If it holds. I think there's a change.' 'It'll hardly break before this evening,' she said. 'Maybe not.' She wondered to herself why his sentences were always so short. Words spilled over in her own mind so much. She had to hold them back, conscious always of his brief replies and afraid she might become garrulous in her effort to fill the void. 'Communication,' she reminded herself sometimes, 'is not only made with speech.' And then she would fancy herself and Joe drawing pictures on the wall, painting excitedly and beaming in satisfaction when they understood each other. The idea so amused her once when she was washing the dishes that she smiled with pleasure. Joe caught the smile as he was passing the kitchen window and asked her about it later. She couldn't tell him. 'It was only a funny thought,' she said. 'You're a queer one,' he said, laughing at her as he went out the door. He wouldn't have laughed if she had told him. He hated to be analysed. Once she had told him crossly that he thought self-knowledge was masturbation, but he pretended he didn't know what she meant.

When he had gone to the creamery, rattling the churns on the trailer over the pot holes on the avenue, she brought the eggs into the kitchen for cleaning. She took out the dish of cooked tripe and onions from the fridge and put it in the oven. He'd like that for breakfast. She liked the oniony sauce, but not the spongy feel of the tripe. She'd have an orange herself.

'Any post,' she asked him when he came back half an hour later. 'Not a thing,' he said. 'Any news at the creamery?' 'Not a word.' It was almost a ritual. She clutched at the few sentences he let fall without prompting, and would sometimes go over them afterwards, savouring each preposition, each monosyllabic word. Once when she had the temerity to reproach him for not talking to her more often, he said she'd have something to grumble about if he was out every night in the local with the boys, or running after some flighty woman who wanted to be run after. She had to agree that it surely would be something to grumble about, but it wasn't a fair comparison. He was just a man, so he said, 'I've got a lot on my mind,' and went away before she could retaliate. She wanted to scream after him, 'I've got a lot on my mind, too, but I need to share it. If I don't share it with you it might be with one of your friends who holds my hand too long when saying goodbye, or squeezes me when we're dancing at the Hunt Ball.' It wouldn't do any good, of course. And she didn't want to start screaming. She calculated that one scream led to another, and she might end up screaming at herself.

'The tripe's good,' he said. 'You always like tripe,' she smiled at him. He had queer tastes. 'You like oranges.' His smile was a reading of her thought. Eagerly she said, 'Are you sure there was no post?' 'Well, nothing much, only the notice about the T.B. Test.' 'Oh. When is it?' 'On Wednesday. He's coming to me first. I'll have to get them in at half past nine.' 'You can keep them in the paddock after milking,' she said. 'I could hunt them into the yard myself while you're away at the creamery.' 'That would be handy,' he nodded his appreciation. 'We'd better move now. Have you the water boiling?' 'I have,' she said, and was glad to be ready for him.

The calves bawled hungrily when they heard them mixing the linseed and boiling water outside the house. She put two measures of the hot sticky mixture into each of six buckets. He lifted the churn of skim milk and filled the buckets almost to the brim. Inside the house the calves jostled for the best position. Two of them got their heads stuck between the bars of the wooden railing and had to have their

noses whacked to make them pull back. They put the
buckets up on the ledge in front of the bars and the first
six fed eagerly. Five times they refilled the buckets, marking
each calf as it finished with a splash of milk. They noticed
the thrivers and looked for scour in the young calf whose
coat had lost its bloom. They were pleased at the success of
their rearing methods and discussed it together. When the
thirty calves were satisfied, they let them out to graze.
Martha scrubbed out the buckets and tankards while Joe
finished cleaning the milking machine and hosed down the
cement floors. It was eleven o'clock. She went back into
the house to do the tidying and prepare their midday meal.
She was tired. She sometimes wondered how her neighbours managed with young children to care for. Nappies
to wash as well. No wonder they looked exhausted. But
happy just the same. A child is a candle in the house, was
the old saying. Her mind created an image of a great golden
candle flame dispersing shadows of loneliness. The sigh
that came from her startled her and made the long held-
back tears spring to her eyes. Stop it, she muttered to
herself. Tears are for townie women with no guts. It was a
habit she had got into, admonishing herself, reminding
herself to count her blessings. And there were blessings to
be counted. She thought back to the struggle they had in the
early years. Even last year. The calves had got blackleg for
the first time and four had died; they lost four from hoose
pneumonia; two from a virus pneumonia, and one calf had
been lain on by its mother. She had cried quietly over that
one. The others she had nursed, bottle fed and injected
with anti-biotics, and it was useless. 'That's farming,' her
husband said. It could be worse, was her neighbour's
comment, a kindly woman who had put twenty years of
farming behind her and knew what she was talking about.
There was no good making a litany of disasters, storm damage, pests, disease, accidents. They had known them all.
This year they were over the top of the hill. Joe had built up
a herd of cows, with his usual patience, culling the poor
milkers ruthlessly, and now they had thirty good Friesian
cows, milking well and all in calf for next February. Every
penny they had went back into the farm, and neither of

them grudged it. Nothing was gained without work, patience, skill. She felt happy again. She left the dinner cooking and ran down the fields to meet Joe as he brought up the first tram of hay from the meadow. He laughed at her sunny face and reached down to pull her up beside him on the tractor. 'Isn't it a lovely day, Joe?' she said, kissing his rough cheek. 'A beautiful day,' he said, kissing her back. He sang, 'Oh Mary this London's a wonderful sight,' with mock pathos, and she knew that he was happy too.

On Wednesday morning she got up earlier. The weather was holding. It was an Indian Summer. There had been no rain for three months. Where the soil was thin over the limestone rocks the grass was singed. The early morning dews prevented a complete parching. Her wellingtons glistened as she walked. 'Hup there, hup there,' she called softly to the old cow who always hung back because her hoof nails were long, horny protruberances and because the young cows would bully her if she went too far ahead. Martha coaxed her along, then ran to head off a few straying heifers. To her right, Joe was bringing up the rest of the herd with the dog, Shep. The sweet tangy smell of early morning fields delighted her. The sun was just beginning its slow climb from the east. A thin finger of smoke pointed to the sky from Cahill's chimney. They were stirring too. Mrs Cahill would be hanging the heavy iron kettle on the crane in the open fire, raking the wood and turf ashes over the kindling until they blazed. She had to milk the cows by hand before she got the children off to school. Her husband's body was twisted with arthritis. Twenty years older than herself, he was an old, worn-out man at sixty-five. They had married late and now had a young family to provide for.

Martha hooshed the last of the cows up to the yard gate. Joe closed it behind them and shouted, 'Thanks a lot,' smiling and nodding at her. A brown curl, with a streak of grey, crisped under his hat. She wished he could have a long holiday so that the hollows and the grooves in his face would fill out. Maybe next year. Surely next year they could manage it. The thought lightened her step and she skipped like a young girl up the back field to start her chores with the hens.

That evening, as she sat rubbing the odd dirt spot off the eggs, preparing them for their journey onto the breakfast tables of the town hotel, Joe said, 'I noticed a few lumps already on the cattle.' 'Oh,' she said, 'that's very quick. We'll have a few down so.' 'It looks like it.' 'It won't matter if it's a few bullocks,' she said. 'We'll get a fair price from the Department for them.'

On Friday morning, the vet came to check his testing. He worked quietly and without comment. She sensed the silence when she came out to them. 'How's it going?' she asked. There was an unusual intensity in the faces of the men in the yard. Joe looked around at her and his eyes slipped from her stare. 'Not so good, Martha, not so good.' 'What do you mean?' Her voice rose a tone, but she didn't care. Pat Meehan, the vet, used a deliberately conversational voice when he said, 'They're all down, Martha, every one of them. You've had a right flare-up.' 'You're pulling my leg,' she said. 'I'm not. I wouldn't joke about a thing like that.' She turned quickly and went into the house. She could feel her jaw-bone contracting in the effort at self-control. She moved hurriedly, getting coffee ready for the men, as if by outpacing her thoughts she could keep that dark cloud of anxiety away. Anyway, there could be a mistake, she thought, and knew that there couldn't. The vet's car started up. They weren't coming in for coffee. She heard him bumping down the avenue. She ran out to help Joe hunt the cattle down to the river field. 'What'll we do?' she asked, childishly slipping her hand into his. 'I don't know in the hell,' he said grimly.

They watched the cattle move easily ahead of them through the open gate, their coats sleek after a good summer's grazing, the cows' udders still showing a fullness of milk, although autumn days were upon them. She recognised the heifers she had bucket-fed from the time they were three days old, remembered how they had bawled helplessly for their mothers, how the cows roamed the fields outside for two days and a night, listening and answering plaintively. 'How could so many have gone down the same time?' 'I don't know,' said Joe. 'I just don't know.'

He drew the last of the hay in that week. As they built it

up in the hay barn, limbs aching and eyes smarting from the seed dust, they knew there would be no gentle cows munching contentedly at it in winter time. They couldn't bear to talk about it, yet each knew that the other thought about little else. Martha wanted to blame someone or something. Had the vet made a mistake the last time and passed a cow he shouldn't have passed who had infected the herd. Even so, five or six might have gone down, but not the whole herd. Was it the milking parlour? Was it the drinking trough? She knew Joe would be going over all the possibilities in his mind, too. When she questioned him about it he was morose and said his mind was buzzing from thinking about it. 'We'll have to wait and see how they kill out.' 'Will they really be slaughtered? All of them?' she asked unnecessarily. 'Of course,' he said, 'all of them.' If she had found a nest of rotten eggs out in the field she might even have believed in the pishogue that someone had put a curse on the farm.

Sunny days following one on another made a mockery of their misery. It was difficult to accept that the brilliance of blue skies could look down on anything other than lovers or holidaymakers, or contented old people drowsing in deck chairs. Nights were diamond bright. When the sun went down, still late and reluctantly, the stars sprinkled the deep blue canopy with luminous spots. Martha and Joe worked doggedly, but now without satisfaction. Aching limbs were witness only of the fickleness of a treacherous world. They wished the cows were gone. Perhaps some primitive instinct for survival made them want to remove all trace and reminder of doom so that they could start clean, from the depths of existence, all over again.

Martha did not cry until one morning when she watched the bully cow elbowing her way to the front of the queue waiting to be milked. She had always reminded Martha of bossy women at sales. In the past it had made her laugh. Now she cried. And for the next three days she cried unrelievedly from morning until night. She lamented not only the loss of the herd, but the wheat crop blown flat by storm, the hay barn they had watched collapse like a pack of cards under the hurricane, the cows that never farrowed, the hens

slain by the fox, the blighted potatoes rotting in pits, the
long-gone dead calves. She cried the way the keening women
cried at wakes over the transience of life, the frailty of
human effort, the weakness of the human spirit. She cried
in despair, and she cried for envy of her town friends who
worried about appearances, good manners in their children
and which part of the continent they would visit for their
next holidays. Joe looked at her blotched face, but could
say nothing that would comfort her.

Her tears were a sedative. The knot of grief loosened
and she took on again her accustomed role of comforter
or silent witness. She coaxed him to eat, but his taste for
food had died. He grew thinner and quieter. The house held
silence in every corner. She began to talk to herself. 'What
really kills me is the injustice of it all. Of course, he wouldn't
think of that. All he'd say is, "Those things happen." As if
that explained it all. Or "That's life." It's as if his whole
philosophy could be cirucmscribed by those two sentences.
I don't accept it. Ten years I've been struggling, doing
without things, never buying a stick of furniture for the
house and doing with hand-me-down clothes from my sleek
city sisters.' She indulged lavishly in alliteration during
these monologues. 'It's not worth it. Life must be more than
an upward climb, with the summit a hole in the ground, six
foot long, and an epitaph, "Here Lies". Here lies all right.
A pack of self-deluding lies. Well, God, if you are there at
all, it looks as if the more patient and tolerant we are, the
more knocks we get. The broader the back the heavier the
burden, or some such idiotic proverb.'

Her monologues were successful therapy. In the past, she
had talked herself out of gloom, neurosis, over-confidence,
inhibition. She could intone her predicament to the sink,
word for word, until it hung there quivering under her
accusing eye, and finally disintegrated with the bubbles in
the dish water. Joe's healing process was slower and perhaps
more painful because he was not so able to articulate his
despair. Their fathers would have said, 'God's holy will
be done,' and slipped the problem easily onto divine
shoulders. Such faith and such relief were not a part of their
lives.

It was on a day in October the trucks came to collect the cows. They were up long before dawn. Martha was sick and couldn't eat breakfast. Joe swallowed two cups of tea. They hunted the cows up to the yard for the last time, through the drenched grass. The cows called to one another in excitement and played games, poking at the ground with their hooves, tossing their heads and frisking elephant-like with one another. Only the old cow, ambling along slowly, scorned such indecorous behaviour. Martha's mind recoiled from images of victims being led to execution, of sad trails of humanity walking innocently into gas chambers, of Abraham with the knife poised over his unsuspecting son, of the sacrificial lamb. She felt miserably that they were adding another flame to the great pyre of human misery which would one day consume the earth. 'They're only cows,' she repeated to herself. 'They don't understand.' And did not believe either supposition.

In the yard the lorries waited. Three men helped them load. As if sensing the anxiety in the air, the cows were uneasy and kept doubling back out of the truck, or dodging around the corner. The men waved their arms and sticks, shouting hoy there, hoy there, goback, goback, goback. The old cow was first to give up, and Martha shut her eyes tightly when she saw her take the first shambling run in. Through the clamour and the excitement there flashed, like a pain to her optic nerve, a recollected picture of pastures yellow with buttercups, of this, their first cow, nudging her newly-born calf onto its legs. So strong was the image that it superimposed itself on the dull, cool morning, and she felt on her face, not the damp wind of an early autumn, but the warm sunshine of the long gone summer and smelled the grass at the full peak of its lushness before seeding. It was the smell of fear from the sweating herd which made her open her eyes and jump to intercept their last break for freedom. The ramp was lifted up and locked into place at the back of the truck. Joe turned his face away and she went back alone to the house.

When he didn't follow she went to look for him. She found him in the machine shed, sitting on an upturned cement block. He was nearly crying. 'If you cried,' she said, 'you might feel better.' 'What's the use of anything?' he replied. 'It's a bloody waste of time. And it's no life for a woman.' He looked at her with sudden perception. 'And I haven't even given you children.' Coming from him it was like an accolade. 'Well, it wasn't for want of trying,' she smiled, trying to tease him into good humour. 'And it wasn't your fault. Look at me. The original biblical barren woman. In some societies I might have a rock tied to my neck and be thrown into a bottomless well.' 'I'd say you'd put up a bit of a fight first,' he said. 'Let's go out and get drunk. What is there left but booze and sex.' 'There's fight,' she said. 'What's life if it's not a fight?' 'We've lost all the battles so far,' he sighed. 'I'll soon be too old to fight.' She put her arms around him, cradling him until he responded. 'We'll never be too old,' she whispered into his ear. 'And we'll never give up the fight until we're dead.'

It began to rain, 'God,' she said, 'you forgot to fix the leak in the roof and the rain will be coming in on my polished table.' They ran into the house, getting basins and buckets ready to catch the drips from the ceiling. 'What did Pat say in her letter this morning?' he asked her suddenly. She looked at him solemnly. 'She said she had to sack her Ayah again, that the heat was withering her roses, and that the Mercedes is in being repaired so they'll have to manage with one for a few weeks.' 'One what?' he asked, astonished. 'One car, y'oul eejit. Very awkward for them.' She began to laugh, and so did he. They sat on the floor watching the raindrops pelting in faster on the plastic buckets, hitting the sides and splashing out on the floor. They laughed at the enormous joke of life, at the huge, side-splitting, star-shattering, cosmic comedy of it all. Then Joe cried for his empty fields and for the poor victims of their last campaign.

THE WHITE HOUSE

by Michael Curtin

Around the time de Valera gave Churchill his answer George Ellis bought the White House. George worked in the Customs and when he inherited a couple of thousand pounds he thought it would be a good idea to buy a small pub. His wife, the former Madge Brilly, was thrilled. They had been married only a few months and the kitchen sink had no attraction whatsoever for her. She was a gay, charming, liberated woman devoted to the Arts, and stolid George was a refreshing contrast to the wild young men who adored her. Now that she was married, running a pub would give her something to do. Characteristically, George continued in the Customs until he was sure the pub could yield a comfortable living. By that time he had discovered he loathed serving in the bar. Particularly with the clientele Madge had amassed. All the customers were either writers, actors or painters or thought they were writers, actors or painters. He decided to hold on to his job and left the pub in Madge's capable hands. He had to help out occasionally at night but his heart was never in it. Still, the extra income was comforting.

Madge Brilly's bridesmaid and fellow flapper of the time was Nan Daly. She was among Madge's first customers. Nan, at nineteen, was regarded as an outstanding local actress.

She was constantly exhorted by all who knew her to seek fame and fortune further afield. She wore a trousers, smoked an odd cheroot and drank a pint as good as a man. Yet there was nothing masculine about her. She was in fact so beautiful that the few men around who might have been worthy of her were so conscious of their deficiencies in her presence that they immediately smothered their desires. Those who made no secret of their admiration were such rubbernecks that there was no danger of their feelings being hurt by a rebuff. Madge was to spend years promoting the cause of every extrovert and deep poet who lent a tone to the bar, but Nan would only laugh and point out that she was waiting for someone more on George's line. When George would be in the bar they would have a great joke about it. Madge would say that Nan could have him – that he had no interest in the theatre, that he was only interested in his golf and rugby – she didn't know how she married such a philistine.

It never occurred to Nan to try and conquer the world. She enjoyed acting – just as she enjoyed singing or listening to one of the pub poets. She had no desire to emigrate or live on beans or be had by an impresario, as she fondly imagined was the statutory apprenticeship of the stars. She was quite happy to put in her day at the office and rehearse at night, or drop in to the White House for an evening with the literati. Now and again she went out with one of Madge's recommendations and sometimes she was kissed. She never went further than that – no one did at the time, at least no one with any sense. These little affairs scarcely ever lasted more than three dates.

Doggie Doyle clarified her emotions. He wore a cravat and was known to be a lady-killer. He was a sporty type but his heart was in the right place and he was drawn to the White House. Madge looked upon his gall as charm and raved about him. He walked Nan home from the pub one night and before she knew where she was he was courting her deftly against the door. He was neither clumsy nor eager and knew when and where and how subtly to massage. Nan went to bed out of breath. She relived her contact with Doggie and found to her amazement she was thinking of

George. It was weeks before she could accept it. She was in love with George. She remained in love with him for thirty years.

On the odd night that George did potter about behind the counter Nan's heart did not beat any faster. This was what she loved about him, she decided. She could be relaxed and natural in his presence. George was unaware of her existence other than that she was a friend of Madge's and he tolerated her as amiably as he did the other odd bods who laid bare their souls in front of the fire. Nan accepted the cruel twist of fate that attracted her to the unattainable. She threw herself into the theatre. When she was not acting she was producing. She had affairs and inevitably, as time passed, she sometimes allowed a relationship to reach its natural climax. She enjoyed herself but always surrendered to the thought that if such pleasure could be had from a liaison with a vacuous artist, what paradise the droll George would surely provide. She did not feel envious of Madge. On the contrary, she was drawn closer to her. Madge had such good taste. Oh George, George!

The golden age of the White House was in the early fifties. Still without bingo and television and sensing the approach of the technological age and its inevitable con-comitant of slipping standards, the people flocked to the bedside of the dying relative – the theatre. When she was not rehearsing or acting Nan Daly held court around the fire. The passage of years had eroded her armour and now in her full maturity she drank like a fish and, her beauty mellow-ing, was more available. But her dream of romance died hard and whenever she did succumb, George still hovered in her imagination in the platonic background. Doggie Doyle had become a bit of an arty buff and brought his sporty friends in with him. They were reasonably well behaved and Madge, in her moments of weakness, wel-comed their presence because they drank a lot and, unlike the pure artist, they had the money to pay for it. The White House was now well known as the sanctuary of every bastard descendant of the Muse incestuously listening to one another's recitations of poetry or snippets from books of the mind.

The gradual decay of progress became apparent in the early sixties and culminated with the invasion of the post-Beatle, battle-dressed, proxy orphans of the Vietnam war. Conversation was replaced with the strident strumming of people overcoming. Sloppy, anaemic, tubercular, draped on high stools, they wailed: 'We shall overcu-uh-um, we shall overcu-uh-um.' The drama group creaked at the seams. The gradual influx of younger members onto the committee was reflected in the choice of productions. Nan Daly, who had wallowed between Coward and O'Casey for almost a quarter of a century, was expected to mother angry young heroes with the vocabularies of sailors. She declined. However much she now indulged herself in private life she would not take down her spiritual pants on the stage. So Nan, Doggie Doyle and the rest of the fading old guard were pushed into the background of the White House, their gentility insignificant amidst the vocal rabble of the media age. But as with all rabble of any age their roots were shiftless and the early seventies revealed the White House camp, jaded and devoid of 'go'. The old guard came back to power, joined this time by a new devotee, Billy Whelan.

Billy Whelan's discovery of the White House had been inevitable. His family owned the local newspaper and a talent for composition at school seemed to pre-destine his career. The paper's narrow spectrum gave rise to the jack of all trades and Billy became a gifted obituarist, critic and sporting correspondent who, with facility, wrote ill of nobody – and despised himself for it. He was clean-shaven, good looking, well dressed and polite – a refreshing change to the White House from the recent trash. Madge was mad about him. Doggie Doyle was thrilled to have him as a source of inside information on the sporting world. He even got on well with George. Nan Daly liked him instinctively but then she was a very easy person to get along with. Billy thought they were a quaint lot and he secretly prided himself on his friendship with them. Not for Billy the world of the discotheque, the speculation about drugs, the naked indulgence in unabashed sex. Only with this vanishing breed could he be distracted from the sense of his own uselessness. He did not know what he wanted, only that he wanted to do better. He acted with the drama group and with little effort he was commendable. Maybe he would become an actor. There was little enough to it, he imagined, except hard work and a bit of luck. Or a writer. More hard work and luck.

Billy did not have a girl friend. He was shy with girls. At least with the girls with whom he came in contact. They were not shy. They could curse and swear with an insouciance they never learned at their mothers' knee. He felt fragile in such company. He dreamed of a maiden whose hand he could hold and at whom he could smile coyly with excitement. He dreamed in vain. The shy maidens were dead and gone, hounded out of existence by the unquiet revolution of bad taste. He noticed old men and women standing on crowded buses; football fanatics chanting obscenities; women polluting conversation by their tolerance of its vulgarity and frequently by their very entrance into it. He smiled sadly at the introduction of plastic milk bottles; they would reduce breakages. Even at his tender age he could recollect when a clip on the ear reduced breakages. It distressed him that people for whom the American Dream had come true and who had houses with seven bedrooms preferred margarine to butter. Every evidence of change for the worse he noted and found himself looking down his nose at the world.

Nan and Doggie and a few other cronies often took drink back to Nan's flat when the pub closed. It was a gathering of the lonely and displaced and although Billy was always invited and sometimes went, they were amazed that he did not seem to have something better to do. Nan felt particularly inhibited by Billy's presence at these late night sessions. It wasn't that in his absence hair was let down or anything of that nature but she felt her fading stature should not be exposed to the young. In the pub, where the talk was general, she lost no caste, but the intimate nature of the late night gatherings highlighted her frailty and sadness. Billy was witty in a cynical way in the pub but his droll observations of the present day merely reminded Nan and the others of their own actual suffering of what he joked about.

There were a few bottles still standing one night when

Doggie and everyone except Nan and Billy had passed their quota. When they had all staggered home poetically and Billy and Nan were alone the drink made her bold enough to quiz him. What was he going to do with himself? Was he going to continue with his obituaries and court cases until he inherited the paper? Had he no desire to go out and conquer the world and all the rest of it? Why hadn't a fine young man like himself not got a fine young girl to look after? Billy told her. He destroyed the local customs and neighbourliness and stultification. He lamented the dearth of women of character. He admitted his burning desire to change the world. Why hadn't Nan – a fine woman, he gallantly conceded – why hadn't she married? Why was there nothing now in her life except tippling in the White House? Was everyone blind that no one appreciated her? Nan laughed. He was a terrible flatterer. No, he meant it, he assured her. The conversation died for a while as they gulped the remaining bottles. Nan found herself talking about George. How she had always persuaded herself that she loved him. Billy only half heard her. He gathered she had never come across the magic person he himself was sure he sought.

Billy blurted out secrets he would never confide to a contemporary. With so much insurance Nan trotted out some of her own peccadilloes. Like youngsters surreptitiously flicking through the pages of a dirty book they charged the atmosphere with their exchange of confidences. Nan was sprawled on an armchair while Billy sat erect and excited on the sofa. He was staring at her and she acknowledged it. She beckoned him but he wasn't sure. She motioned her head again and this time, though still unsure, he rose and stumbled over to her. She drew him to her and they slipped slowly down the armchair onto the floor.

Billy was still asleep on the floor when Nan went out to work. He woke with dry lips and a cigarette cough. He remembered everything and blushed with the recollection. He threw water on his face and tidied himself as best he could but he was a nervous wreck at work that day and the usual platitudinous speculations flew anything but freely from his typewriter. When he finished late that night he knew he needed a drink badly but he was afraid to go into the White House. Yet he knew a drink anyplace else would make him worse. The usual crowd, including Nan, were there before him. Nan was as relaxed as ever and greeted him as though nothing had happened, but he wasn't his usual witty self. Nervously he spoke when he was spoken to and when he tried to engage Nan's eyes she avoided him. Apparently it had been a drunken bout and no more. He had better forget about it like a true sophisticate. But he couldn't forget about it. For days he relived it and after a week, fortified once more by drink, he followed Nan home from the pub. She stopped when he caught up with her.

'Can I come up with you?' he blurted out. She nodded.

They vowed that every night would be the last night. They felt as remorseful as two teenagers tempting fate. But something grew between them gradually that was more than the sum of what they had mutually to offer. Finally, through tears, Nan said one night: 'I love you Billy Whelan. Oh God, I love you.' There were no more maidens for Billy to hold hands with and smile coyly at with excitement and for Nan there was no George in the platonic background.

And then Madge died.

She died with little originality, suffering an early morning stroke while stacking up the shelves in the pub. A pensioner in for his constitutional malt found her. The newspaper office was just around the corner and Billy heard the news within the hour. He rang Nan but she had already known and had gone to the pub to see what she could do. Billy made a few more phone calls and a large gathering were soon on the scene protesting to one another that Madge had seemed in great form the last time they saw her. The efficient undertaker set plans in motion to have her boxed by the night, and the death notice, together with a hasty appreciation from Billy, appeared in the evening paper. He would do her justice in the weekend edition. Nan looked after the bar during the day and when they took Madge to the church that night Doggie Doyle went behind the counter. There seemed to be a tacit understanding that the White House should not close on such an occasion. Billy, Nan and Doggie served the bar after the funeral. The place was crowded. George was there. He felt he had to be there with these people keeping the pub open for him. Although he couldn't understand why the pub shouldn't be closed. Maybe Madge would have wished it open, as they said, but he didn't know. It was most peculiar. People he had never met came up to him and shook his hand and told him they knew her well. Acquaintances Nan hadn't seen for years turned up. It was more than Madge's wake – it was the wake of a way of life long since dead but only now interred.

She had a huge funeral the following day but what with pressure of business and various other excuses only a hard core went back to the pub. They had no pressure of business or if they had they said to hell with it. Madge Brilly was dead. Or Madge Ellis as she is now. Or was. George faced up to his responsibilities. If the pub didn't close yesterday there seemed little point in closing it today. Although he would have to hire someone to tend it. He couldn't have that bunch turning it into a poets' co-op. Nan took the death very badly. She got so drunk Billy had to carry her home. He did it without the subterfuge they normally resorted to as though he was performing a corporal work of mercy and had nothing to hide. He had to put her to bed and felt the increased intimacy that such a personal deed effects.

Pathetically George installed a farmer's daughter as barmaid. She was coarse and insensitive and was constantly rebuked by Nan for spilling drink or forgetting to put briquettes on the fire or humouring the knobs of the old wireless to a pop music station. They grew testier every day at the sight of her and when George dropped his bomb-shell it was a welcome relief. He was selling the pub. An auctioneer pal of his had a client. A returned exile who had spent ten years in the States as a contractor. He felt he could 'make a go' of the place. On the last night they presented George with a hastily commissioned drawing of the pub, gratefully executed by one of the younger artists who appreciated the opportunity to make some recompense for the slate that had died with Madge. George thought it was a nice gesture. Obviously it was the thought rather than the unintelligible impressionism of the sketch that counted. He stood to the house and there was much drunken speech-making.

The new owner was friendly in the uninhibited American way. He had a distressing habit of constantly cleaning the counter. Little by little he effected small improvements. He blocked up the fireplace and put in a gas fire. He tantalized them with his contemplation of which corner would be most suitable for a colour television. He had a lovely transistor that had access to BBC One, Two, Three and Four. The old wireless with the face like a chapel door, from which Dev's voice once rallied the nation, stood silent in the background. Finally he closed the pub for renovation.

The White House was closed for a month and Nan and Billy and Doggie no matter where they went could not feel at home. When it reopened the exterior was scarcely affected. A coat of fresh paint brightened the Tudor facade. Nan opened the door with a sense of anticipation. The high stools were gone. Every place she looked she saw covered leather seats with little tables in front of them. She blinked at the gaudy colours of the television. Billy was standing at the bar watching her stocktaking. She walked towards him and noticed, over his shoulder on the wall where the old posters advertising the drama group used to hang, a splendid dart board. Her face coloured and her lips trembled. 'Good Christ,' she said.

There was a complete reversal in their relationship. Up to now Billy had been ever eager and impatient for the rendezvous in her flat but with the death of the White House Nan began to need him more. She consumed him. She rang him during the day, something she had never done before. She brought him into the flat earlier and made him stay later. The natural outcome was that Billy's enthusiasm began to wane. It was grand to drop into the White House and pick her up when he felt like it but meeting her in other pubs where their relationship was obvious and the atmosphere less liberal was another matter. Luckily Nan sensed what was happening and she had the maturity to know what to do. On a night when he was in a particularly hot mood from drink she refused him.

'What's the matter, Nan?'

'I want you to do something for me, Billy.'

'I'd kill a dragon for you, Nan.'

'I want you to go away.'

'Go away? Now?'

'Yes. This very minute. Tilt your hat at a rakish angle on your head and hop on a boat. Go away and become a dishwasher or an elevator operator or sleep in a telephone box or whatever is the thing to do. Go away before I drag you down with me. Do you understand?'

'You're tired of me. You want to cast me aside and take up with someone else.'

'Billy, I'm serious. Give up that crummy job and go away and become something.'

When he realized she was in earnest the words began to go to his head. She flattered him outrageously about the talent he had. He could become a great writer if he broadened his horizon and gave himself a chance to develop instead of contracting in the arms of an old hag. Billy was glad she had the character to bring it out in the open. He knew he would have to leave sometime – leave Nan at any rate; they were being whispered about in pubs. They talked till four in the morning. Nan assured him she would manage quite well without him. Billy did not know whether he should make a final overture.

'Do you want me to stay?' he asked. Nan shook her head.

He paused at the door for a minute and said: 'Thanks for everything.'

Nan forced a smile. 'If I was only your age what a great time we'd have.' She said it airily. He could not think of a suitable reply. She motioned her head for him to go and, relieved, he blew her a kiss.

After he left she sat folded in the armchair, chain smoking, and letting ash fall carelessly on her breast.

IN ADVERSITY BE YE
STEADFAST

by Patrick Boyle

You don't work as a farm labourer for
twenty-five solid years, day in, day out, fair weather and
foul, without getting to know the peculiarities of your
employer. And Andrew McFetridge is a queer duck surely.
The neighbours claim he's a dour, thin-lipped Presbyterian,
greedy for money and too mean to spend a fluke on the
jollifications they themselves indulge in. But that's not the
whole of the story. He's certainly a hard-driving boss who'll
work the guts out of you from dawn till dusk. Still he won't
ask you to do a job he wouldn't tackle himself. And the
pay is good. No, all's wrong with the man is that he has a
bee in his bonnet about religion.

Now religion is a funny bloody thing. It is a bit like the
drink – most people can take it or leave it alone: the odd one
becomes an addict. And you can safely describe Andrew
as a religious addict. It is his belief – a fundamental article
of his faith – that any kind of relaxation is sinful and merits
the wrath of God. He neither drinks nor smokes. Never in
all his sixty years has he set foot in a dance hall or cinema.
In his farmhouse you'll find no such works of the devil as a
radio or a television set. Not even an old-fashioned gramo-
phone. And there's neither chick nor child about the place,
although he's married this many a year.

As you'd expect, this way of life does not encourage neighbourly traffic. So the evening when there comes a loud knock at McFetridge's back door, there is a stir out of no one in the kitchen. Andrew, who is sitting at the big open hearth-fire, easing off his wellingtons, stays motionless, one boot held up like a question mark. Over by the dresser, the wife, Jane, stands glowering, a finger to her lips.

There is no second knock. Instead the latch clicks and a man's head is poked round the door.

'Evening folks. Hope we're not intruding.'

You'd know at once by the soapy voice and the big black Bible tucked under his oxter that he's one of these travelling preachers. A Holy Roller. Or a Dunker. Or maybe even a Mormon. Without as much as a 'by your leave' he comes sailing into the kitchen, followed by his mate, a much smaller man, carrying a class of a leather case.

'Is this where Andrew McFetridge lives?' says the tall man.

Andrew deposits his wellington boot on the floor.

'Aye,' says he.

'My name is Bryson,' the preacher says. 'And this,' he points, 'is a fellow worker in the vineyard of the Lord, Brother Clarke.'

Jane is quick off the mark. She clears away the unused dishes, already laid on the bare kitchen table.

'We were just sitting down for a mouthful of tea,' she says. 'You'll maybe join us.'

Without waiting for an answer, she gets out the damask tablecloth and the tea set and the swanky cutlery and the silver teapot – wedding presents kept under lock and key – and she starts setting the table in the new.

'We were told in the village that you were an upright God-fearing Christian, Brother McFetridge,' says Bryson.

Jane by now is fluttering around, pulling out chairs from the table.

'Will you not sit down?' says she.

'Thank you, Sister,' he says. 'We just stopped by to see if you would join us in invoking the blessing of the Lord Jesus on both your labours and on ours. A short family prayer session.' He gives a pious sort of giggle. 'A cup of tea when we are finished would be most welcome.'

Andrew frowns. You can see he is embarrassed.

'We'd be glad to join you in prayer,' he said. 'Only –'

Bryson eyes the dishes on the table and the kettle singing on the hob.

'We could call back later if we are disturbing you,' says he.

'Oh, no,' says Andrew. ' 'Deed you're not disturbing us in any way. It's just that,' he jerks his skull as if he were heading a ball, 'James here isn't one of us.'

'Didn't the Good Lord say: "In My Father's house are many mansions"? There is shelter for every man, be he Baptist, Presbyterian, Methodist, Anglican –'

'He's a Roman Catholic,' says Andrew, as though he's just after donning the black cap.

'No matter,' says Bryson. 'We are all brethren in Christ, gathered here together to seek the blessings that only heartful prayer can obtain.'

'Hallelujah!' says Clarke, the first time he opens his trap.

Andrew clears his throat.

'Well, James,' says he. 'Would you like to join us?'

Would a duck swim? Sure a man would have to be a born idiot to forgo a chance like this. Don't people say that at these prayer meetings they roll about the floor, grinding their teeth? Or go into a fit of the shakes? Or even tear their clothes off? And forby all that, going home now would mean missing up on the tea.

'Och, sure there could be no great harm in saying a mouthful of prayers.'

'Very well,' says Andrew. 'Close over the door, Jane.'

As the ould one goes to the door, the cat comes in from the yard, saunters across the kitchen floor and settles down at the fireside. A big brute of a white Persian with its hair trailing the ground, it scowls at the assembled company as though accusing them of trying to hold a religious service in its absence.

Bryson starts leafing through the Bible.

'Now, folks,' he says, 'I am sure there is no need to remind you that if you are seeking help or guidance or consolation, you have only to go to the Book of Psalms. David has the answers to everything. So we will begin with a reading from Psalm 23.'

The chairs are pulled back and the company gets to their knees around the kitchen table. For a few seconds the preacher stares up at the ceiling like you'd see a missioner doing in the pulpit, until the coughing and the rustling and the shuffling have died down. At length he starts reading from the Bible.

'The Lord is my shepherd: I shall not want.'

A class of an agricultural discourse, no less! The care and rearing of black-faced sheep. Specially laid on for mountainy slobs.

'He maketh me to lie down in green pastures:
He leadeth me beside the still waters.'

Green pastures, how are you! And still waters! Little the big fat gulpin knows about herding sheep on the side of a mountain. With grass as scarce as gold dust and water-logged bog-holes waiting to swallow up the unwary. Not to speak of snow and storm and the depredations of hunting dogs at the dead of night. Oh, 'tis far from the Sperrin Mountains this man of God was reared.

He goes on reading about restoring souls and walking through Death Valley and a lot of other tripe, and then he comes out with:

'Thou preparest a table before me in the
presence of mine enemies.'

Believe it or not, those are the preacher's exact words. Not satisfied with persuading a poor bugger to take part in a sectarian gathering, he starts rubbing in the fact that the table you're kneeling beside is laid for the tea and that damn the bite you'll get till they're finished with their bloody ould abracadabra. And on top of everything, reminding you that your enemies are gathered about you, smacking their lips over your plight. Oh, there's no doubt about it, there's little change in this country over the last few hundred years. But what can you do except soldier on and hope that the acrobatics will start before you're destroyed with the hunger.

You'd think he's reading your thoughts, for the next thing he comes out with is:

'I will dwell in the house of the Lord for ever.'

And it looks bloody like it, for he closes the Bible and starts a long harangue about the value of prayer. Making contact with the Lord Jesus, he calls it. You would think he's a radio ham the way he talks of switching on the infinite power of the Creator, getting the right wave length for salvation, tuning in to the Only Begotten Son and babbling away about frequencies and modulations and faulty elements and now and then – cute corbie that he is – getting back again to the sheep farming with the odd reference to slaughtered lambs and wandering sheep and a daft remark about 'the mountains skipping like rams, and little hills like lambs'. You'd wonder that anyone – let alone a clergyman – could come out with such a load of crap.

Andrew is kneeling up very straight, head askew, face ploughed up into a ferocious frown as though he's having trouble sorting out the meaning of the preacher's words. And no wonder. A mountainy farmer, so thick that he won't give house-room to a wireless set, is hardly likely to make sense out of high frequency prayer. Much less hills lepping around like little lambs.

The ould dolly is crouched over a chair nursing her chin on her clasped hands and gazing into space. Every so often her empty stomach sets up a growling protest that would rouse your sympathy if you weren't feeling worse yourself.

But Brother Bryson must be preaching on a full stomach for he keeps gabbling on, regardless of grumbling guts and scowling faces and dying fire.

At last the sermon ends. But does that conclude the proceedings? No such bloody luck.

'And now, friends,' says the preacher, 'we will invoke the pity and clemency of our Heavenly Father. And what better way to preface our supplication than the first few verses of Psalm 102?'

He throws back his head, the eyes rolling in their sockets, and addresses the rafters.

> 'Hear my prayer, O Lord, and let me
> come unto Thee.
> Hide not Thy face from me in the day
> when I am in trouble:
> Incline Thine ear to me: in the day
> when I call answer me speedily.'

He has the whole thing off by heart, rattling it out like a nursery rhyme, only taking an occasional skelly at the open book.

> 'My heart is smitten, and withered like grass
> so that I forget to eat my bread.'

D'you hear that? He has a brass neck on him! Making out that he has hammered at you with his exhortations till the spit has dried in your mouth and the hunger gone off you.

> 'By reason of the voice of my groaning
> my bones cleave to my skin.'

Well, you can say that again. The sight of the food on the table and you kneeling so close is enough to rise turmoil in anyone's guts. Though no doubt the preacher would claim it is the Word of God that is driving the burps out of you.

On and on he goes, blethering about pelicans and owls and house-sparrows; stones and dust and grass; indignation, wrath and drunken weeping; you could make neither sense nor meaning out of it. 'Twould put you to sleep instead of giving you the Holy Roller shakes. Indeed, looking round the company you can see that they are all beginning to show signs of wear and tear. Jane is yawning her head off. Andrew's eyes are closed, his head hanging, his body swaying backwards and forwards. He's flogged out after a hard day's work. And ready for nothing but bed. Even the cat, sitting up proud as a bloody pasha, is squinting at the dying fire with drowsy, slitted eyes.

And now Brother Bryson is in full cry. He has closed the Bible and is waving it aloft, extolling its wisdom and prescience, its reliability as the answer to all the troubles of the world – fear, loneliness, anxiety, discouragement, sorrow and weariness – its indispensability to the Good Life

102

and the ultimate crown of salvation, its significance as the corner-stone of the Christian faith. He drones on, with Brother Clarke chiming in with an occasional Amen or Hallelujah and the old lady's yawns becoming more audible and the cat settling down for a comfortable snooze and Andrew snoring gently as he teeters back and forth, until –

Suddenly his body sags and he slumps forward, his head fetching up against the table with a crunch that would put the heart across you. The preacher breaks off in the middle of a sentence. Dead silence for a couple of seconds.

Then, like a drunken man gathering himself together, Andrew pushes himself back from the table and squats down on his haunches. There is a dazed look on his face and a lump on his forehead the size of a duck egg.

Jane jumps to her feet.

'Andrew,' she cries, rushing over to him. 'Are you badly hurt?'

The two Bible-thumpers join her.

'That's a nasty bump you got, Brother McFetridge,' says Bryson.

'Still it didn't draw blood,' Clarke says.

Andrew looks at them dully. He draws a hand across his forehead.

'Och, 'tis a thing of nothing.' The bruise is now as big as an orange.

'He could have split his skull,' says Clarke.

'Will you not sit down?' says Bryson pulling up a chair.

'Should I put a poultice on it?' Jane says. 'Or would it be as well to get a doctor?'

Andrew eyes them irritably.

'What's all the fuss about? Doctors and poultices and sit-down prayer meetings? Over a bit of a clout on the head.' He squares his shoulders and draws himself up, clasping his hands together again. You have to hand it to Andrew. No half measures about him. If there's praying to be done, it must be done regimental fashion.

'Maybe there's a bone broken,' says Jane. 'Or some damage to the –'

'Get down on your knees, woman, and let the Reverend get on with his discourse.'

'But you wouldn't mind a poultice? It's only to keep down the swelling.'

'Nonsense. I'm as right as the rain.'

Fighting words, all right. But the voice is kinda squeaky. And he has gone very pale in the face.

Jane thrusts her hands out in a gesture of despair.

'He'll pay no heed to me,' she says.

Bryson leaves his Bible down on the table beside a plate of oat-cakes that would put you slobbering with the hunger. He turns to Andrew.

'Brother McFetridge,' he says earnestly. 'Our little prayer session is concluded.'

Andrew gapes at him stupidly.

'Concluded?' he says.

'Yes. We can omit the usual closing hymn.'

But Andrew is not taking surrender terms from anyone. Clerical or lay.

'Indeed and you will not. Not on my account you won't.'

The preacher glances across at the old dolly for guidance but she shrugs her shoulders helplessly.

'Very well,' he says. He clasps his hands and gets in touch with the rafters again.

'Abide with us, dear Lord,' says he, 'for it is towards evening and the day is far spent.'

He has the neck of a giraffe. If it hadn't been for himself and his butty, the tea would be long since over and the company well on its way to dreamland.

'Brother Clarke,' he says. 'The closing hymn.'

Your man grabs the leather case, places it on the dresser and opens it up. A blast of music fills the room, rumbling, thundering, booming. It must be some sort of a recording machine.

Andrew and Jane are listening open-mouthed and out of the tail of an eye you can see the cat standing stiff-legged, its back arched in terror. And why not? For the poor brute, no more than its master and mistress, has no conception of the wonders of amplified music.

The next bloody thing, pandemonium breaks out. A male choir, assisted by the two preachers, are bellowing at the top of their voices: 'Abide with me: fast falls the eventide.'

Above the clamour can be heard the screeching of the cat as, roused to panic, it claws its way up the bricks of the fireplace. Lucky enough, the fire is nearly dead so it comes to no harm. But as it disappears up the chimney, Jane comes to life and starts screaming.

'Oh, the cat! The poor cat! It'll be roasted alive.'

Andrew is leaning against the table, his hand to his forehead. Bryson, who has been conducting the unseen choir, stands with his hands raised in a papal benediction. Clarke is clutching his mouth as though a note has stuck in his gullet and he's in danger of puking. The machine is still belting out the hymn.

'When other helpers fail, and comforts flee,
Help of the helpless, O abide with me.'

Somewhere up the flue of the chimney the cat is howling, the sound muffled but quite audible above the uproar. Jane darts across to the fireplace and, in the lull between verses, calls up:

'Pussy! Poor old pussy! Come down, will you. Come down.'

Her voice is nearly drowned out with the choir starting up again.

'Swift to its close ebbs out life's little day.'

You can hardly blame the bloody cat for staying where it is with all these strange voices bawling out in unison that it's gone closing time so drink up your drinks don't you know it's after hours the premises must be closed and have you no homes to go to.

The old girl is worried to hell about what's after happening her pet and she starts wringing her hands and shouting blue murder.

'Will somebody do something. Do something will you. Don't just stand there gaping. Do something.'

The two preachers rush over to join her and the three of them crouch around the hearth, shouting up the chimney:

'Pussy! Pussy! Pussy! Come down, Pussy. Puss! Puss! The naughty puss. Come down, pussykins. You can't stay there all night.'

105

Damn the bit heed the cat pays to their exhortations. No more than it does to the mechanized hallions now roaring:

'Through cloud and sunshine, Lord, abide with me.'

If the muffled yowling is any indication, the poor brute is up near the chimney pot by this time, with every intention of abiding there till the coast is clear.

This possibility dawns on Jane, for she straightens up and turns to Bryson.

'The roof,' she says. 'There's nothing for it but the roof.'

'How do you mean,' says he. 'The roof?'

'You'll have to get up on the roof. It's the only way to reach the poor thing.'

You can see that Brother Bryson has no stomach for this caper. He starts back-pedalling at once.

'Maybe we should try just once more,' he says. 'To see if it will come down.' And then, as an afterthought, 'What name do you call it?'

'Eh?' says Jane.

'What name does it answer to?'

'Pussy, of course. Or sometimes, Puss.'

'Has it no proper name? Like Felix? Or Blanche?'

Jane is getting impatient.

'You don't give Christian names to cats. Come on,' says she, starting for the door. 'I'll show you where the ladder is.'

The choir is still going full blast when she comes back into the kitchen but she pays no attention. She makes straight for the fireplace, where she starts calling up the chimney.

'Are you there, Pussy? Oh, good! We'll have the poor old puss cat out of there and safe and sound in a few minutes. There's two good men gone up on the roof to take you down.' She swings round. 'Isn't that right, Andrew?'

Andrew, hands grasping his knees, is sitting up very straight on a chair. But his face has gone a class of grey and you can hear the clatter of his teeth above the sound of the recording machine.

'What's wrong?' says Jane, dashing over to him.

'I'm cold,' says he. 'Bitter cold.'

She runs a hand across his forehead.

'He's done for,' she wails. 'Och, God help us all, he's done for.'

After all these years she should know her husband better. Sure there's only one way you can hurt a tough old cormorant like him and that is through his pocket-book.

'Stop your whinging, woman,' he says, 'and throw a sod or two of turf on the fire.'

So away with Jane to the creel at the hearth side where she gathers up an armful of turf and starts building up the fire again, her ears cocked to the chattering teeth of the boss and paying no heed to the crying cat or the noise of the preachers on the roof or the choir bawling:

'I fear no foe with thee at hand to bless.'

But the bloody fire won't light and Andrew is getting impatient.

'What's keeping you?' he says. 'Can you not get the fire going?'

You can see the old birdie is rattled. She glares around, looking for kindling. Spots a bottle on the dresser. Grabs it up and darts back to the fireplace. The screw-top seems to be jammed and as she is struggling to release it a voice is heard from the chimney. It is Brother Clarke.

'I can't reach far enough,' says he. 'You'd better try.'

You can hear them shuffling about on the roof. Changing places carefully. And then Bryson's voice. Very clear. As though he has his big head poked into the chimney pot.

'I see the little fellow. There should be no trouble getting him out.'

Just then Andrew lets a groan out of him. Not a groan of pain, but of irritation. He has come to the realization, not for the first time, that you must do everything yourself. That a woman can never be trusted to handle anything. He tries to ease himself off the chair.

'Here,' he says, 'give me that bottle.'

But Jane has been roused to a flurry of action. The top of the bottle is off. She is splashing the contents wildly over the dying fire.

It must be petrol she is using for suddenly there is a WHOOOOOOSH, and a sheet of flame rushes up the chimney.

107

After that it is pure bloody Bedlam. From the old dolly a scream. From the rooftop a roar of pain, ending in what sounds awful like a well-known expletive. From the cat in the chimney a muffled howl, mounting to a screech as it loses its grip and tumbles down the flue, to land, tail ablaze, in the hearth.

For a split second it crouches there, blazing tail threshing back and forth. Then, like a shot off a shovel, it starts careering around the room. You know how the squib they call the Jumping Jenny behaves when you light it – leaping madly around and banging against walls and furniture. Well, that's the way the cat is performing, only now and then it starts whirling around with the sparks flying off it as though it is giving an imitation of a Catherine Wheel. The long hairs of the Persian breed make ideal bonfire fuel, so by the time it dashes out the open door into the yard, screeching blue murder, the poor brute is ablaze from stem to stern.

The company is too stunned to make a move or say a word. But overhead you can hear Clarke's awestricken voice:

'Hey, look at the cat! It's on fire!'

Between grunts and moans, Bryson can be heard casting doubts on its ancestry and expressing an unChristian disregard for its ultimate fate. These sentiments seem to rouse Jane from her stupor, for she starts rushing to the door.

'My God!' she says. 'The poor creature!'

She is soon pulled to a halt.

'The tablecloth, woman!'

It is Andrew. He has struggled to his feet and is pointing with outstretched hand. He appears excited. And who would blame him. In its fiery exit, the cat must have brushed against the tablecloth. Now the draught from the open door is just starting to set alight the smouldering material. It is confined to a single fold of the cloth and anyone with half an ounce of wit could quench it with a clap of the hand. But Jane, the poor slob, yanks the cloth and its precious burden off the table and, in her excitement, stamps and grinds and tramples it into submission on the floor.

You would nearly find it in your heart to feel sorry for

Andrew. There he stands, a look of horror on his face as the full extent of the catastrophe dawns on him. A pedigree teaset, cutlery of the best, a damask tablecloth and a valuable silver teapot, the only surviving relics of the past, maybe never before put to use, now lying smashed and damaged and scattered on the kitchen floor. Not to mention that he is going weak in the knees and the cold sweat is rising on him and the lump on his head is still swelling from the bang he got only now it has started throbbing like an old-fashioned threshing machine and he is so hungry that he'd eat his way through two ends of a dunghill and he is dog tired after a hard day's work and if everyone would only go home he would clear off to bed and he wishes to goodness that the choir would lower their voices a little for it is driving him completely crackers. Mouth open, he is about to make his protest when the commotion starts up overhead. The two preachers are banging on the roof-tiles and bellowing at the top of their voices:

'Fire! Fire! Fire!'

Andrew stumbles to the kitchen door and you can hear his gasp as he realizes that his hay barn is ablaze. The flames are roaring up sky-high and you can hear the hiss and crackle as the fire spreads through the tightly packed hay. Above the sound of the fire, and like a class of an accompaniment, the choir is chanting:

'Hold Thou Thy cross before my closing eyes,
Shine through the gloom and point me to the skies.'

You would think they were deliberately making a mock of poor Andrew's reaction to this final catastrophe. For in the glare from the fire you can see him leaning against the door-post with his eyes closed as though he doesn't want to see what is happening. It is a cruel sight, to say nothing but the truth. Jane is over at the pump in the middle of the yard, her arm going like a fiddler's elbow as she drives the pump up and down. The two preachers have collected buckets and are running backwards and forwards, shouting encouragement to each other as they try to throw water on the flames. With the heat, they cannot get near enough for the water to reach the fire. But even if it did, it would have as much effect as the squirt of a tobacco spit.

The fire has a right hold now over the whole hay-barn and in its light you can see the bruise on Andrew's forehead pulsing and his lips murmuring. You'd gamble the last tosser in your pocket that what he is muttering about is the un-desirability of house-cats, the crass stupidity of wives, the doubtful value of travelling preachers to the evangelical cause, and the folly of carrying thrift to the point of refusing to insure your hay barn against fire. You would be very wrong. For if you incline your ear close, you will hear him repeating fervently in time with the choir:

'In life, in death, O Lord, abide with me.'

A FAMILY OCCASION

by Emma Cooke

It was a Tuesday afternoon and the family was coming to tea. The parlour in 'Sunnyside' was fragrant, polished, waiting. Mrs Lee's chair stood, with its cushions nicely plumped, beside the wireless. In the fireplace a small flame licked its way around a sod of turf. The black marble clock on the mantelpiece coughed and struck three.

The Girls, Dodo and Polly, were home from England on their annual holiday. They had travelled from London on the previous Friday. They were upstairs getting ready. Dodo had filled the cut-glass vase on the bookshelf with roses and carnations. A posy of pansies, pinks and forget-me-nots stood on the pedestal table by the window.

Mrs Lee was in bed having her afternoon nap; dreaming that she was bringing the children on a picnic and that Polly and Dodo, who were unaccountably grown up, had taken Beattie away in the pram.

Lucy was in the kitchen counting the iced fancies that had been sent over from the confectionery. If Beattie brought all her brood, which of course she would, they were going to be short of a cake. She sighed and opened the box with the sponge sandwich in it. She cut a slice and added it to the plate of buns. She would do without her own slice. The act of self-sacrifice replaced her annoyance with a warm little glow.

111

Now to start the potato cakes. She had just enough time.

At half past three Lucy untied her apron and put it away, looked into the small mirror beside the cupboard, patted her hair into place and went into the parlour. Her mother was already sitting down, wearing the new black cardigan that The Girls had brought home.

Polly and Dodo appeared, elegant in pinstriped suits, tailored blouses and immaculate ties. Polly looked at the clock. 'Nearly time,' she said. She and Dodo lit cigarettes. Lucy took one as well. She only smoked when The Girls were home on holidays; by herself it felt wicked.

Mr Lee looked at them from his photograph on the mantelpiece. He had taken it himself – two years before he died. Now that she was in her thirties the resemblance between himself and Dodo was very pronounced.

Peg arrived before their cigarettes were finished. She swept in all twitters and gaiety, her two children, Barbara and Stanley, following shyly behind her. Like The Girls, she had a neat figure, sallow skin, dark glossy hair. But her style was softer. Her hair was permed and today she wore a dress of navy blue and white striped material with a little floppy bow at the neckline.

'My goodness. She's all dolled up, isn't she, Polly?' said Dodo.

'Chase me Charlie!'

'Look who's talking,' cried Peg, 'you're very swanky yourselves.'

Lucy watched them, thinking how close Peg and The Girls had always been. She hoped that Beattie wouldn't be too late. Beattie was so disorganized.

'How are Barbara and Stanley?' asked Polly.

The children hung their heads.

'Stanley, button your blazer,' said his mother.

'And Barbara has her school uniform on,' Lucy pointed out.

Barbara was brought forward to show The Girls her brown coat, the special pleat in the front of her gym slip, the zip pocket, the cream blouse.

She stood like a dummy, trying to hold onto the feeling

112

of superiority that her first year away from home had given her. But it drained away under her aunts' scrutiny, leaving her as vulnerable as a snail without a shell.

'How do you like Dublin?' Polly inquired.

'She loves it,' said her mother.

'Ever get lonely?'

Barbara shook her head.

'Good girl.'

'Are you fond of each other?' asked Dodo, who knew very little about children. Barbara and Stanley nodded. The women turned away from them with a sense of duty done, and began to talk all at once.

'Can we go and play?' Stanley called shrilly to his grand-mother. Mrs Lee nodded and they escaped to the garden.

The hands of the church clock stood at five past four. Beattie shoved and pushed the children past the gate. They always wanted to stop and look at the tombstones. Organ music pealed inside. A funeral march. Mr Watson practising. Someone must be sick.

'We're late for Grannie, Barbara and Stanley will be there already,' said Beattie. She had a stitch in her side from rushing and the new corset. She was sorry now that she had left the baby with Mrs Green. She could have put Michael and Dickie up on the pram.

'Hurry, hurry, hurry!' she puffed. Mr Everard stood at the door of his shop. Hands behind his back, eyes half closed, not a speck on his white tennis shoes. Nothing to do except watch the world go by. Everyone except herself seemed to have time to spare.

'I want to see Barbara,' said Yvonne, who was the same age.

'Good,' said Beattie. Over the bridge and round the corner. They were nearly there. Surely the children had been a lot tidier when they left the house, thought Beattie. Sometimes she wished that she was like Peg, with only two. She wondered how she was going to last the afternoon in her corset. At least it might keep Dodo from noticing that she was pregnant again.

Last summer, when she was home, Dodo had called up

one afternoon and sat through a complete ironing session; talking about England, and theatres and friends that she had made, while Beattie tried to fold sheets and dresses so that the torn parts would not show. Before she left she placed a brown paper parcel on the kitchen table, saying cryptically, 'I don't want to interfere.'

Beattie opened it as soon as Dodo had gone. It contained a book called *Planned Parenthood*. Beattie had been annoyed at first. But then, knowing Dodo, she giggled at the funny side of it. She put the book on the top shelf of the wardrobe where Seamus would not find it. It was still there, gathering dust.

The children waited for her on the front step of 'Sunny-side'. The door was always on the latch and she pushed it open.

'Yoo-hoo!' she called.

An echoing call came from the parlour. She went in, the children straggling after.

'Ah! Beattie – at last!' said Mrs Lee.

'And all the chick-a-beatties,' added Polly and Dodo in unison.

'One, two, three, four, five –' counted Dodo.

'Six is with Mrs Green,' Beattie said quickly.

'– six, seven, all good children go to heaven.' Dodo crinkled her grey eyes.

'The whole family, Beattie. How lovely.' Auntie Jane, who wasn't really an aunt, was there because The Girls were home.

'Not quite, Auntie Jane,' Beattie said.

'Goodness me, I lose count,' said Auntie Jane, wafting lavender water with every gesture.

'I knew you were here, I smelt you through the door,' five-year-old Dickie told her triumphantly. The Girls smothered their laughter.

Beattie caught his arm. She could have murdered him. 'Tell Auntie Jane you're sorry,' she demanded.

Dickie looked at the carpet. 'Sorry,' he whispered. He wondered why it was rude of Auntie Jane to smell so pretty. He liked it. There was a short pause to let his apology register. Then Mrs Lee said, 'Barbara and Stanley are in the garden.'

The children tumbled out of the room. The Girls clapped their hands over their ears in mock dismay.

'Go easy!' Beattie yelled. 'Sorry Mother,' she added automatically.

Lucy stood up. 'I think I'll put the kettle on,' she announced, 'Frank will be over from the shop soon.'

'Can I help?' asked Peg.

'Thank you dear, but I know where everything is,' Lucy said apologetically.

So do we all, thought Beattie, sitting down on the sofa beside Auntie Jane. Everything in 'Sunnyside' had been kept in exactly the same place as far back as she could remember, down to the chocolate egg on the top shelf of the bookcase. It had been there since she was a little girl. A present from cousins in America. She remembered, when she was small, wishing and wishing that her mother would take off the cellophane wrapping and divide it up. Let them see what it tasted like. But she never did. It must be mouldy by now.

The women settled down to a comfortable chat about the things that had happened during the past year. Frank came over from the shop and when he went back to sit in his office, Desmond, the younger brother, arrived.

'I suppose it's all gone,' he said when he came in.

'Every scrap,' said Polly.

'I'll go and squeeze the teapot.' Lucy bustled out to collect the pile of potato cakes that she had been keeping warm for him.

Frank leaned back and rubbed his waistcoat after he had eaten six. 'Well that's more like it,' he said.

'Do you remember the day that we went on the picnic down the river and you gobbled up all the buns? You must have been about five years old,' Polly asked him.

'How many were there?' he prompted her.

'Twelve!'

'Oh my!' said Auntie Jane, her eyebrows nearly touching the brim of her hat.

Desmond guffawed – then, 'Do you remember the time

that Frank gave Peg a carry on his motor bike and her knitted skirt caught in the wheel?' he said.

The memory convulsed the room.

Dodo took over. 'How about when Lucy fell down the grating in the church aisle?'

'I was going in to do the flowers for the Harvest Festival.'

'And Percy Ward had lifted the grating back to get down to the furnace.'

'The rector had to come and help pull her out.'

'Lucky she's well padded.'

The stories were told, one voice taking up the thread from another. Beattie shifted on the sofa. A bone from her corset was killing her. The room seemed very warm.

In the garden the children played their annual game of pelting each other with the small, unripe apples that had fallen off the trees. This year Barbara and Yvonne were the targets. They crouched in the greenhouse waiting for a chance to make a dash for the big laurel hedge.

'I'm getting a new coat,' whispered Yvonne as they peered out through the tomato plants.

'I'm learning ballet,' said Barbara.

'What's that?'

'Dancing, of course.'

'Oh!' They both tried to look nonchalant.

'Everyone learns –' Barbara was interrupted by a volley of ammunition from the enemy, who had decided to try a surprise attack.

'Come on!' They clasped hands and ran squealing through the doorway.

She was going to die. Here on Mother's sofa – after all they had done for her – in return for their tolerance – she was going to, at last, as they had always expected her to, commit a final, unforgivable breach of taste. Sweat drenched her armpits. She tried to smell it, distending her nostrils, her lungs aching for a whiff of some antidote to Auntie Jane's lavender.

'Do you really, Beattie? Imagine.' Auntie Jane was looking at her in amazement.

116

'Oh yes.' She bared her teeth at them, but nobody seemed to notice anything strange. What on earth were they talking about? The melodeon? It was quite true. She did lock herself into the kitchen and play it for half an hour after she had put the children to bed. Yes, if someone was still crying when she stopped she attended to them. She sat there nodding while the family recounted the details.

'Young people are marvellous nowadays,' gushed Auntie Jane.

A miscarriage would be worse than dying. Think of the mess. Poor Lucy would have to do all the work. But she couldn't have a miscarriage with Desmond still in the room. Mother would never allow it. If she was dying they'd have to send for Seamus – and the priest. They'd never think of the priest and Seamus would have a fit. She hoped Seamus wasn't drinking today. She'd have to make her last confession in her mother's parlour. Oh God!

'It's your own personal decision, Beatrice.' That's what her father had said. He had been a just man. He used to stop her on Sunday mornings when they met. Walking opposite directions to church. Both of them alone. Lucy was the only other churchgoer in 'Sunnyside' and she got up for eight o'clock. Seamus always went to last Mass.

'Good morning, Beatrice.'

'Good morning, Father.'

'Are you all well?'

'Yes, thank you.'

They might have been heads of state exchanging credentials. It often struck her as comical. But he wasn't a man for frivolity.

She felt dizzy. She wished that she was in her own house. She wished that they could afford to get their wireless fixed and then she wouldn't need the melodeon. Seamus had taught her to play it when they were courting. She wished –

Wails, reaching a crescendo as they approached the sittingroom, halted the conversation.

'Oh dear!' Peg half rose to her feet. The Girls blew long spirals of cigarette smoke. Lucy got up anxiously.

'Some naughtiness, they're as wild as young goats,' said Mrs Lee, looking accusingly at Beattie. Desmond hid his

117

grin behind a handkerchief as Lucy hurried from the room.

'I'll help her,' Beattie said. She wrenched herself out of her agony. The pains went through her heart as she stood up. But she made it to the door, only knocking a bowl of flowers to the ground on the way.

It was not the end of the world after all. Barbara's uniform was a bit muddy and Yvonne had a nasty scrape on her cheek.

'What were you doing in the hedge anyway?' asked Lucy, brushing away at Barbara's brown serge. Beattie had rushed upstairs muttering something incoherent.

'Playing,' they said vaguely.

Beattie came into the kitchen and took a sheet of brown paper from the pile in the left-hand cupboard.

'What's that for?' Lucy asked.

'A secret,' Beattie replied airily. She hurried out again and they heard her singing 'ta-ra-ra-boom-de-ay' as she climbed the stairs.

'What's she doing?' asked the little girls.

'Goodness knows.' Lucy shook her head. There was never any accounting for poor Beattie.

In the bathroom Beattie wriggled out of her corset. It was a hideous pink thing, with numerous laces and silver eyelets. If Seamus saw her in it he'd have a fit. She rolled it up in the brown paper and hurled it high onto the top shelf of the hot press; back behind the eiderdowns and winter curtains. A surprise for Lucy when she found it.

She stood in the middle of the bathroom floor and felt herself relax and expand, like a flower about to bloom. It was marvellous. Funny to think that she was a grown woman. She remembered the time when her chin was only a few inches higher than the rim of the bath. Sometimes the whole thing seemed preposterous – the children, babies, Seamus.

Funny how she had met Seamus. He had drifted into a social in the Parochial Hall. A stranger in town. Not knowing that he was trespassing. Masquerading under false colours at a Protestant dance. He had been sent to work in the region by the Turf Board. Everyone had been delighted

118

to see a new young man turn up. When the rector's wife came over and introduced herself the truth dawned on him. He decided to bluff it out. It would make a good story for the lads.

Beattie had been standing near him at suppertime.

'Jesus!' The expression had surprised her. She had turned round to find Seamus standing staring at a sandwich as if it was about to explode.

'What's wrong?' she asked.

'What day is it?' he murmured.

She looked at the clock. It was after midnight. 'I suppose it's Friday,' she said.

Seamus looked at her in horror. 'And I'm eating meat,' he said. He often said later that the first thing that had attracted him to her was that she was such a good sport.

They danced together for the rest of the evening, the offending sandwich tucked away in Beattie's handbag. That was a joke that she had kept to herself. In the end it hadn't been funny at all.

A button like a little gum drop rolled down her dress and rested against her shoe. It was followed by another.

'Beattie,' a voice called anxiously, 'where are you?'

Beattie stooped and picked them up. Lucy would have a needle and thread. Dodo was outside on the landing.

'For heaven's sake, Beattie, what are you doing?'

Beattie held out her hand. 'Look!' she said.

Dodo peered at the buttons, then at Beattie's gaping dress, then at her flushed face.

'Oh Beattie,' she said, 'you're not –'

Beattie nodded her head. 'I am.'

'Honestly, you're hopeless.' Dodo looked at her with concern. 'I get worried about you,' she went on, 'when I come home and see you with all those children, and that man –' she broke off. 'Can't you do anything? Can't you be more careful?' she asked in a dry, matter of fact tone.

'No,' said Beattie, 'we're not allowed.' There was no point in going into all the details, but when she said it out like that, to her sister, it seemed ridiculous.

As they stared at each other Beattie felt a soft flutter in

119

her stomach. It was the baby. The first time that she had felt it moving. She placed her hand protectively against her body. 'I'll be alright,' she said, 'keep your fingers crossed.'

'Wait,' ordered Dodo. She went into her bedroom and came out carrying a cardigan. 'Put that on, it will keep you covered.' She placed it gently across Beattie's shoulders.

They linked arms as they went downstairs. In the parlour everybody turned expectantly towards them.

'What's up?'

'We thought you were lost!' the family exclaimed.

'Beattie burst her buttons,' Dodo announced. And the way that she said it made it sound so comical that they all began to laugh.

LOVE–WAR

by Patrick Burkley

     Fergus waited in the Vintage Bar nearly half an hour. There was no sign of Miriam turning up. He heard in his noble head the rapid, complaining voice of Mr Healy say, 'I don't care a damn if he's a good family. He's a bad influence. Four o'clock.' The gloom and phoniness of the pub – bits of old cars ornamenting the walls – seemed consciously to deepen depression and turn the mind to drink. The establishment was a dark place of ill-repute in a provincial community where all reputation tended towards the worst, the darkness perhaps designed to suggest a fashionable rusticity by interior decorators down from Dublin who succeeded in conveying only the kind of melancholy they experienced in a rural pub.

    Officialdom, in the emaciated form of a restless barman wearing a dirty white jacket, viewed with elaborate disfavour the silent patron's working-clothes or perhaps the arrogance with which he moved in housepainter's overalls, being an artist. Fergus sat by a small round table where meals were served, a cold lunch and, presently, a sort of tea to justify a long gold-coloured neon flashing into the dark the red legend: The Vintage Bar Traditional Lounge & Diner Come for the Crack! Music booze plus grub! Prop. Mrs Nash.

121

It was a small town and the barman knew him. They had been in the same class in the local Christian Brothers.

A couple of dowdily dressed American girls came in and sat on the low high stools. They spoke in a muted, humanist tone, egregiously tender. 'What became of Caspar?' one suddenly shrieked and both laughed as if lightly tickled. They ordered whiskey.

'Sure, absolutely sure, you got no rye?'

'No, ah, none of that here.'

Fergus approached the counter and stood a little behind them, dividing, silencing, beginning with a glum air so that any actions relevant to his prey might make them aware that they were waking a great being from provincial indifference. He drew himself up to his full five feet eleven and a half inches. This generated an interesting air of authority to which the girls paid no heed. They gazed into each other's eyes and smiled. Presently the silence broke down, a crackling in her throat like the sad reluctant start, the first playing in years of an old record:

'So she said I had to pay for breakfast ate or not. I said that's a crazy law.'

The girl who spoke wore jeans and a scarf enfolded her hair, an old red scarf as if life were one unpleasant chore. While buxom she was tall and vibrated from a firm waist and from big restless shoulders an aura of impregnable melancholy. The sight of her evoked a sad athletic young man filling tax-forms, anxious to fling the documents out the window and to vent his anger on an oval ball. The other girl's face, basically plain, wore an expression of furtive amusement when she smiled, which she did in fits, a fat face, red and fallen, red with health and red again with shame. Her slight body bonily parodied the vague hunch of the big girl's shoulders. A nice girl, Fergus thought, body too bony, face too fallen. To his circle of friends he'd freely remark that he liked his tail big.

The big girl spoke of her nightdress and shortly of astrology. 'I know I have medium powers,' she said. The other nodded nervously, in spasms, before the purpose of each sentence emerged. Another of my rare tastes, Fergus thought, I like women who talk a lot, it expands the sense

122

of power, the power to shut them up. Poor fat face. Definitely out. A light of sanctity shone thinly in the dark red embarrassment of her cheeks. Closer inspection also discovered that her forehead bore a small dent in the middle, darkening earthly prospects. With old-fashioned eccentricity, she wore a skirt, a wrinkled cotton article, apparently found on a rainy bush. She looked at once conservative and prostitute.

'A vodka,' he said. Fergus enjoyed more than the drink its sophisticated association with the plain people of a foreign country.

'Saw you painting the other day,' remarked the barman, pausing before the middle word as if seeking a polite synonym for some mild obscenity. 'The ol' mill by the ol' bay.' His round lips and his round frightened eyes hardly moved as he spoke with his neck elongated, head raised, to cure a stammer.

Fergus wondered whether to play the complete artist or the proletarian bit: he painted sentimental pictures for American and British explorers surveying their cultural empires, seeking affirmation of their homely glory, pictures that these girls, being intellectual tourists, might well view with horror. They recalled in warm pitying noises an encounter with a local soldier. As to the proletarian image – he wore an elaborate cap – Fergus was just a disconnected member of the rural bourgeoisie. His father sold a large farm: a vain ape, in physical aspect a pregnant gorilla, he expanded his fortune yearly and his mind contracted at a similar rate. He was a spectator incapable of thought, a builder who destroyed and a man of massive intolerance who called himself a letter. Fergus's conversations with this delightful gentleman focused on the length of male hair and, their sole mutual obsession, the dogtrack. So that his imagination dwelt daily on patricide and suicide, which was why perhaps that divine faculty was rarely exercised in his art. His most successful painting was an abstract work on the drowning of the Colleen Bawn.

'I only paint walls now,' he said, trusting that his emphasis on walls might imbue the word with a faintly intellectual echo. 'That was my last painting. I'm shagged to death of art.' Good, he thought, I am at once a philistine and a genius. He leaned heavily against the counter. 'You know, Joe, painting's a queer business.' He made a circular motion with a loose wrist. 'Disorientates.'

'I had an uncle,' said Joe, 'a terror for the books.'

The big girl turned round slowly and gave two short laughs, if a trifle sinister vaguely favourable to all this quaint expression and to Fergus's artificial dilemma – for Fergus knew neither painting nor life, but proceeded to agonize on the subjects to the barman who said, 'I don't know, I'd like to be able to paint.'

A greyhaired van-driver came in drunk and played a slightly out-of-date record on the yellow jukebox.

Mary Hopkins sang: 'Those were the days, my friend, we thought they'd never end, we'd sing and dance forever and a day . . .'

'Powerful tenors long 'go,' muttered the man, swaying as he gazed at the stone floor. He had apparently pressed the wrong button and remarked that the poor man's voice was gone to hell. A former engine-driver, fired for his involvement in a pseudo-republican mail theft (the charge concealed under alcoholism), Finbar Cronin distributed lemonade when he wasn't drinking – a pity the colour reminded him of whiskey. Fergus said, pretending to be drunk, 'Art as we know it is kaput.'

'Why do you say that?' asked the big girl.

'The I.R.A.,' roared the van-driver.

'O.K.,' said the barman.

'Because I'm an artist and I'm entitled to hate what I do well.'

'What kind of paintings do you do?'

'Works of pure genius. Oh, in all humility only I burn-ded the lot.' He flourished an arm over his head, in a more decisive if equally inelegant strain as the drunk, who appeared to conduct an imaginary orchestra and for late entries to threaten them with republican fury. The jukebox played The Drinking Song from The Student Prince.

'Oh,' said the girl.

'A trip, are you?'

'Yeah well, a trip, yeah.'

'Intellectual refugees. Wasn't that what's-his-name's

saying about what's-his-name? Pascal. René Pascal. Fleeing the Nixon terror, I guess.'

'Now. Vodka.'

'Oh well, Nixon.'

The barman said. 'Are you mixing in?'

'An evil man.'

'You bet.'

'And what is the capitalist system demanding for this conventional narcotic to which it drives us?'

'Twenty-seven.'

'We'd love to see Dingle.'

'All wild out in Dingle,' said the man. 'Mind out. They're all wild bar the women.'

'There's Jansenism in Dingle,' Fergus said.

'Gee. I mean Jesus.'

The van-driver shuffled back to the juke-box and began to sway over the machine like a priest seeing a bright vision on the cold slab of his penal altar.

The big girl and Fergus fell to fruitless conversation on the iniquity of her country, simply articulating common thoughts, the girl giving a little leap of her upper portions when he expressed an opinion particularly familiar to her, as if they'd combined to make a momentous discovery. Rain pelted against the tiny window and its stained glass. The aromatic dust known as compact powder on her face mingled its scent with the whiskey in her breath.

The clip-clop of the riding school passed down the alley beyond the single window, coming from its mountain-trek. 'Pure Joyce,' she said thinking of the dray-carts on cobbled quays, the cry of Dublin seagulls, a city roused to a dull day. She remembered her dead father, a psychoanalyst who wore Donegal tweeds and a big white moustache. Yes, she thought, I loved Paw but then great women do. Pity I read Sartre. Made me give up writing. Him and Joyce. Guess I won't ever really complete Paw's book. An Anatomy of Joyce's Unconsciousness. Love to live in Dublin. Why do I think in this verbal way? Have I assumed a one-way current of consciousness? People just don't naturally think like this. What's this guy, this too beautiful nut, going on about what Thin Lizzie and Horslips? Who the hell's

Thin Lizzie? Sounds like a drag artist. Christ, I'm uncouth.

'Oh, Horslips.' She slammed an open palm against the black counter of Kilkenny marble. 'Didn't they . . . Aren't they some kind of . . . ?'

'They're fantastic,' Fergus said, tone-deaf, hoping the cliché might irradiate the darkness between them, like garish bulbs over a country carnival. The glow of familiarity quickly faded in her eyes and her spirit vanished in resurgent gloom.

Presently they exchanged names, the girls with an air of self-mockery. He ordered drinks all round.

'Caroline,' said the big girl, a Zen Buddhist and an existentialist who hated all names but she hardly hated Caroline although uttering the word with a sneer. 'Caroline, he wants to know what you do.'

Caroline laughed. 'What I *do*?'

The van-driver started to sing, winking at his elevated glass, 'Nothing could be finer than to be in Carolina in the morning . . .'

'There's only one thing wrong with Caroline, she wears these hick skirts. Christ, they're nearly as awful as her legs,' and she pounded her companion between the shoulder-blades, exacting a surprisingly loud and hollow sound of one so frail. Caroline, the big girl explained, was a female suborderly in a San Francisco mental home. If he really must know.

They all grew drunk. Politics arose. Each confessed to 'socialism' as to an obscure vice but as every political party in the world called itself socialist little fruit was borne of the subject and a silence descended as if they'd all remarked that they were bipeds.

'Socialism,' he roared.

'God, the drink's telling quickly,' muttered the barman, tilting his close-cropped head suspiciously as he studied loose change. Fergus had paid for another round. 'We'll win the day,' he said, appearing to hold the counter at bay with an outstretched arm. His head down, he gave an artificial gasp.

The sincerity and extent of Fergus's socialism lay in the persecution of the bar staff in the town's oldest hotel with demeaning remarks on their sex-lives. He was a sexual snob and a vulgar one.

A slight, pervasive and ephemeral excitement seemed to wake his body when he proclaimed his politics or when he announced himself a humanist.

'See that,' he said, gesturing with vague drunken grandeur towards the van-driver. 'That's the kind of man I admire. My idea of a man. We'll win through. By God we will.'

'Oh well,' the big girl said, 'all thinking people are socialist now.'

'Thought is power.'

'I guess so.'

He spoke of modern philosophy, recalling names from The Plain Man's Guide To The Great Philosophers, a work he'd stolen from a Limerick bookshop. Then he denounced W. B. Yeats.

'We *do* Yeats.'

A lady in green evening dress mounted a dusty platform in a corner of the small room and began to play the harp as if its strings contained an electric shock.

'They murdered James Connolly, the Irish re-bell,' she sang, with obscene refinement, quietly dropping final Rs like old embarrassing friends.

She was succeeded by a gentleman equally artificial in a threatening strain, bawling out lusty ballads as if shouting into the face of a dishonest solicitor.

The place filled. American tourists, garage mechanics, insurance agents, a delegation of Dublin skinheads, intellectual layabouts and a few girls generous with their virtue cast tired looks on tired looks. The van-driver, a vaguely familiar figure to Fergus, started an argument with a smiling farmer. 'You stupid bugger,' said the farmer and pushed him to the floor where he banged his head and began to groan, an eerie, childish sound. The girls helped him up.

He was approaching sixty, perhaps, a well-built man with the profile of a Spanish aristocrat and a white toothbrush moustache.

'I'll get the I.R.A. on that bastard,' he shouted the moment he came round. Apparently he looked on the organization as his bodyguard.

'Here, help him up, here, here's your drink,' the big girl said.

He placed a great oil-black hand on the faded seat of her blue jeans. The silent one supported his rise by taking an arm round her neck, appearing at first to genuflect, the help unnecessary, the man obviously strong.

Finbar Cronin gazed suspiciously up. He saw the long hair and brown melancholy moustache of Murty Scanlon's son, the pis artist. The wretched whore was blocking the circulation of his blood, long bony fingers dug into the muscle of Finbar's arm.

'God, thanks,' said Finbar. 'I can get up myself. But listen, ye'll have a drink.'

'Oh, there's no need for that.'

'Ah, we're a hospitable race as long as ye're not Englishmen. Ye'll have . . . What is it the women drink? Wine or something, some class of a drink like your man over there.'

The barman bowed slowly.

Fergus said, 'All right, Mister,' in the accent of a stock Chicago gangster, 'we'll order six quid of cheap wine and you see who hits the hay first. We'll see who hits the floor.'

'I will not,' said Finbar Cronin, 'Guinness is my only man. Up the Ivys. My father was actually from Dublin, you know. Did I ever tell you the story . . . What about, Mister big-time and your wine, how would you fancy a competition based on stout now? Listen, the ladies, what'll the ladies have now?'

'I guess a pint.'

'I'll have a dry Martini,' said the silence.

Fergus slammed five pounds on the counter. 'Twenty-four pints of Guinness.'

A buzz went round the crowd and the music died away.

They drank with savage concentration. After the sixth pint, the van-driver gave up. 'Eire, pure effing childish,' he said and went away to vomit.

Fergus ended up murmuring poetry and roaring politics. He perceived that the girl he hated was in love with him. She must be an idiot.

He said: 'I'm stuck in this hole. Ah, cops want me all over.'

128

Caroline gave a quick sideway nod.

He weighted and clouded his local accent. 'I spent the bloody inheritance in a year, from the mother, you know. Old man cut me off. Bastard. Records and brandy. I've the biggest record collection in Munster. That's me. I'll die in style. I will, though. Working out this infallible odds system. Ah, a man must stand up. Listen, I'd love to ask you back.' He explained Mr Dempsey, his resident landlord, a perpetual drunk and notorious moralist, who was easy on the rent if you sat up in his kitchen all night listening to his views on juvenile decay. Fergus was really drunk now but the still small voice of propriety spoke with elocution in his soul, his dead mother's sharp voice and Mr Dempsey humming in the background. A few nights previously, Mr Dempsey discussed the Oedipus Complex, which he had recently discovered. In the crowded bar his mind went blank. What to talk of. What to talk of. What were we talking about. Anything we were talking about. Connect. 'Is Bowie for real?'

'Say he's the new Presley.'

'What do they think of Pollack now? Has he gone out?'

'Oh, he's in another age, now.' Then she said, 'Veronica, maybe better get the tent tonight.'

'You talk to that Mrs Phelan pervert. I'd only tell her go shit.'

'She likes me.'

Fergus said to Finbar: 'No hard feelings.'

'Life's short, boy.'

The youth placed a hand on the man's far shoulder, a cramped gesture, and said, 'God, weren't you the hard man now to survive the way you fell,' speaking for some reason obscure to himself in a proletarian Dublin accent.

'I was picked up,' the man said in a similar accent. He gave a hard, dry laugh. 'Look at all the immorality now for you because there's a night of culture on the T.V. Did ye ever visit Sweden? I imagine with the advent of the E.E.C. we'll rationalize ourselves. But now, speaking personally, don't get me wrong, I'm not for this business at all, I'm for an independent country. I'm just saying that everything, well most things anyway, bring some good. You must rationalize. Listen, where are ye from?'

'Originally Minnesota.'

'Minnesota, faith.'

'You are cute,' the big girl said in the way she taught children to spell cat.

'I'm cute all right.'

Caroline said: 'Suppose Caspar's actually rowing to California.'

'California, here I come,' Finbar sang. All laughed.

'Time, gents, please,' the barman said, his voice combining menace and fear. 'Time, now. Come on. Time. Time. Ah, time, lads. Lads, time. Lads now time. Now lads time. Time lads, please. Lads please. Lads time now. Lads now, look at the cut of the clock.'

'That was so ugly,' Veronica said, 'that violence.'

'What we need in this country's a strong man go beating up any of these looderamawns go round assaulting, assaulting decent people. You'll always find it's the bostoon, the side of the mountain always at the bottom of it. And they pick on me when you're drunk. What does an urban intellectual like Conor Cruise O'Brien know about the way you can't take a drink down here without some dressed-up bogman carting you off. Urban intellectuals. There's an expression you never thought an ordinary, ignorant individual like myself would be liable to produce. What are you?'

'Am I?'

'Politics, girl, politics. What do you think? Do you believe in a strong man.'

'Nixon is weak.'

Then Veronica bought a carton of Guinness and a bottle of Powers for Finbar.

'The wife,' said Finbar, 'she'd have my life only she's dead. The neighbours say I threw her but I was blind drunk and they may be right. What with looking in windows we know more about the house next door than we know our own.' They stumbled down damp glistening side-streets towards the edge of the town. Fergus leaned on Caroline who slouched along with a vacant embarrassed grin. They kissed once and she said, 'Oh hell. You know, orientals don't kiss. You're like Caspar. He's like Errol Flynn. It's kiss and kill. Each man kills the thing he loves. I think he was the greatest poet of all time. Don't you think he was the greatest?'

Caroline with a tiny fist pounded the door of Ave Maria until the proprietress slowly opened it displaying first the tip of a poker and while Finbar staggered onward with Veronica's support, the slight hunched girl screamed magnificently at the fuming Mrs Phelan until one by one the nearby houses lit up.

'Do you want to wake everyone up?' the landlady said.

'Up the Republic,' the van-driver roared, staggering and embracing in the middle of the road, disturbing the peace of respectable people in grey seedy houses. The whole area was awake. A draper's accountant started from a nightmare of Egypt, about to break open a glittering box, containing gold or a corpse perhaps, in the dark interior of the Great Pyramid.

Veronica said: 'Up Conor Cruise O'Brien,' her big voice cracking.

'And who is this intoxicated gentleman and the droopy moustache by him?' the landlady asked in her doorway. Fergus perceived, beneath curlers, face-cream and a light pink dressing-gown, an embittered bird-like widow who once played bridge with his late mother. The woman's eyes narrowed. 'I know you,' she said.

'Ver . . . at least Car, Caroline, you have ev, everything?' he said, swaying. 'Yes,' she said and handed him a tent. 'I have everything.' And they stumbled down the grey garden-path, a broken tricycle seeming to conspire with Mrs Phelan in her moral views and to menace their passage to sin.

The landlady stared after them, fancying that she might break, with the power of her small dark eyes, the youth's proud back.

The stars glittered coldly on the vacant road, reflecting in the glisten of a brisk drizzle as tired lamplight shimmered in its midst.

Long after the door of Ave Maria closed loudly with contempt, when the landlady dreamt of vanished film-stars and Finbar dreamt of hell, as Caroline's fingers played lightly on his spine Fergus heard the small, harsh voice defeating time and space. 'I know you. I know you.'

The voice pursued him through his dreams and in the morning, as every morning, he woke to the wail of the timber-yard horn.

BLOW-BALL

by Desmond Hogan

What was it for, why was it they came? Perhaps because it was just there, the house. Perhaps because she might have been there, the lady, and she was in a way their object of pursuit.

The house was Georgian and summer languished around it. The fields beyond had a greenish feel, laid with hay cut just as it was turning colour. Men, separate, unobtrusive, were working in the fields and here and there were sprays of poppies. On the pond in front of the house was an accumulative growth of water-lilies: still, strange to the children.

They were drawn to it in a group. Bubbles, whose hair was as bog-cotton with the sun in it. A ragged ribbon fell on her forehead. Hanging over them, keeping her apart from the others at times was her class background. But she was vital because summers were blanks; something had to be made out of them. This required imagination, a special talent almost. Bubbles above all had it. Pee-Wee was gentle then; he drooped at the shoulders, an unawareness about him. There was a department in his mind where the word was fantasmagoria. He was undertaking a study of ghosts. Dony reached him through his oddities, because of them he was Pee-Wee's best-friend. Dony was thirteen, the oldest.

There were others, their younger brothers and sisters whom they brought with them. Other children who trailed along but never really committed themselves. Also Bubbles' English cousin who had buck teeth and told Bubbles' mother sometimes that she had been with the boys. But none of them mattered. Bubbles, Pee-Wee and Dony were the instigators.

They had it to themselves, the house. It looked so contained. In a way it was just like going to the pictures. Pictures which showed sleek skies and coral swimming pools which made phosphorus trails of smoke when someone dived into them, the sort of pictures they went to see. At the pictures love was something important. The house made love important too. It had a mythology of sex, of violence, of the supernatural evolved from the generations of landowners who once lived in it. There was a book written about it, written by a lady of the house, Lady Loughbown. That was the name of the house, Loughbown. The children knew how the lady looked. There was a photograph of her in the book, a photograph of the ghost-like figure in a tapering Edwardian dress. They liked to think that she was buried in the grave in the garden. But most people said it was her dachshunds which were buried there. Pee-Wee wished to see her ghost. Bubbles and Dony wanted to get through to her too.

The book itself had black covers and they usually brought it with them. They took a delight in the suggestiveness of some of the phrases, phrases like 'We were very attached to one another.'

To one side of the house the framework of a greenhouse had broken down into a bed of nettles, among the trees nearby were sleeping crab-apples. The visits to the house were always somehow ineffectual, there wasn't much to do. They'd stand by the pond, they'd stroll about, looking at things. Sometimes they brought food and had picnics. Bubbles could never bring anything more than milk and brown bread and butter. She always frowned when she produced them, did nothing more. On one of these occasions it began raining. They sheltered under a rug in the garden, eating bananas, the rain beating down ceaselessly.

It meant laughter and pulling. The smell of girls' knickers. Total madness.

Often as the others searched about Bubbles and Dony would sit by the pond and talk. They'd talk about the future. Dony intended to be a priest, and go to Africa. Bubbles had an extravagant wish. She was going to be an actress.

Bubbles was a peculiar girl. Unconsciously she imitated adults in her way of talking, in her way of walking, in her smile. After seeing a film she managed a hint of the star in her demeanour.

Sitting by the pond like that she'd brush Dony's hair in the way she liked to have it. She always carried a brush and a comb in a funny, worn bag. There was no explanation for it.

When Dony changed to long pants that summer it was really Bubbles he wanted to see him in them. She seemed to understand. It was just she who mattered. Her family wasn't important. It didn't matter that her uncle had been in court for interfering with young children. It wasn't even important when everybody knew that her older sister shamefully had twins. Her sister went to England afterwards. Dony was at the station when she was leaving. There were two trains, one going to the sea, the other to Dublin. Dony was going to the sea with his mother, to a day of candyfloss, of green ebbtide, of cold. The girl was going to Dublin. She was a bulky girl, in a pink cotton dress, lying against the wall. She looked mute, a little hurt. Bubbles was there to say goodbye to her and she eyed Dony. Dony sensed disdain and rejection on his mother's brow when she glanced their way.

But she couldn't have suspected his friendship with Bubbles. She couldn't have suspected that he'd be with her the following morning, that he was with her almost every day of the summer. They were fugitive hearts, all of them.

But nothing happened to them and they were impatient. Their refrain became: 'I wish something would happen.'

They were baffled when suddenly, unexpectedly, summer was almost over. Their sensibilities changed, the pang of schooldays so near again. More children joined their group, others followed them to the house, spying on what they were doing.

One morning at Loughbown Bubbles decided to do something climactic. She fell on the terrace with a little yelp. She let the others help her up. Her eyes were round and deceiving.

'I've seen a lady,' she said. 'She was all white.'

'It was her!' Pee-Wee started.

They wanted to know more about the lady but Bubbles was vague. All she could remember for them was that the lady had seemed to call her, seemed to have beckoned to her.

They believed because they wanted to believe. It would have been a breach of trust if they hadn't. But Dony said bluntly to her: 'You're lying!' Bubbles looked at him, her eyes begging. It was as if he'd said something irrevocable. 'I'm not!' she cried.

She turned, letting out a little sob and ran down the steps to the stone seat beside the pond. She was apparently transfixed there, her hands hiding her face. Pee-Wee went and put an arm around her, the others standing back ineffectually. One of the younger ones was crying now too; she said she'd seen the devil at a window.

The group was split. They drifted home separately, no need to hurry. It was already long past their lunchtimes. They'd be scolded at home, interrogated for the truth. But their parents wouldn't understand the truth anyway.

It was warm as Dony ambled home, bits of fluff blowing across the lane as if they'd been released from somewhere. He turned as he heard a cry from behind. It was Bubbles who couldn't get over the gate. He went back and helped her across. Her hand felt so tiny as he tugged it; it was white and complete. They walked home together, a little quiet with one another. Bubbles was wearing a pinafore, her head inclined from him, something on her mind.

'I didn't see a lady,' she admitted, 'I'm a liar.' Her voice was just a suggestion, soft. 'I wanted to make you notice me,' she added. Dony wasn't sure what she meant, what she was hinting at.

She spoke about the colour of his eyes, the colour of her eyes, other things, her words slurred. She lowered her eyes and smiled shyly when she said: 'You're the nicest boy in town.'

Coming near her house she pressed his hand suddenly and left him.

The next week they were back at school and they had few opportunities of seeing one another. They depended on chance to meet. Often they encountered each other in the library, the two boys and Bubbles. They were usually bundled in mackintoshes and they'd speak behind a bookshelf. The librarian's eyes would glance at them sporadically. These moments were memorable, mellifluous; the light strained from the rain outside, winter evenings mostly wet.

Once Dony found himself sitting in front of Bubbles at the pictures. It was a picture in which Ingrid Bergman was having a love affair with Humphrey Bogart in Paris. Ingrid Bergman's pale, clear, Nordic face was touched by a Paris lightness. Bogart brought her for a drive to Normandy, a chiffon scarf about her neck, tied out in two wings, fluttering in ecstasy.

Sometimes Dony caught Bubbles' eyes and it might have been that they were sitting together. They really enjoyed the film for that. But already things separated Dony from the previous summer. Awful nightmares, a new recourse in sex; carnal dreams. Pee-Wee was smoking. He'd merged with a group of boys and hadn't much time for Dony.

Somehow he failed to meet with Bubbles for a long time after that and in Spring her family emigrated to England. She called him into a yard one evening to tell him. She'd changed, she wore earrings, very tiny, very minute ones; her hair was in a bun. It was during Holy Week. There was an array of old tractors in the yard, a broken-down threshing machine. The fields about were rimmed by flood water; something inexorable about it. It made Holy Week more real. One strange remark Dony remembered from that conversation: 'Wasn't Jesus very good to die for us,' Bubbles had said.

She suggested they go to the house, to Loughbown, before she went. But this would have been ambiguous now and it was never achieved.

If it had been at any other time that Bubbles went they might have made it dramatic. But summer was almost forgotten and her departure was of little significance. She just slipped away.

AGES

by Eithne Strong

For two or three years it was to be noticed that Jim Donegan veered around Mrs Deborah Owens. The knowledge must have pleased her while she appeared to remain cool, undisturbed in any part by him. During this period he was to be seen, time to time, with girls nearer his own age. She showed no jealousy of them, being apparently indifferent regarding him. She was indeed fully occupied; from her preoccupation she might have given occasional thought, a little smug, to the removed aura in which he saw her, idealized, wife to Derek Owens, senior to him by some grades. The gulf between his idealization and the fact of him; then the husband, of whom he appeared to be in for he remained, even if not entirely unexpressed, on the perimeter of her circle. There were evident things to keep him from approaching the centre: first, she was unneedful of him; then the husband, of whom he appeared to be in some awe; and of course the family, always watchful, aware. He seemed shy of them; possibly he was afraid of the tongues of the clever older beautiful ones.

Then little by little a careful inward movement slowly progressed. Very gradually he verged along a shortening radius, the result being that Jim Donegan and Deborah Owens went together to films. His spoken reactions to them were arranged mostly in agreement with hers. Yet he was someone known to think for himself – he was already reputed to have voiced radical opinions that bothered the entrenched in his profession. But he deferred to her, giving the inference that he considered she was immensely lived, experienced, had wisdom in certain areas that he coveted. She acted as if she had the wisdom not to be over-flattered by this totally positive-looking attitude. There is the other side to this homage, she possibly calmly told herself, there always is; some of him must surely see me as just a bag declaiming.

They went to concerts. He was considered something of a mind on music which she was not, yet he gave every evidence of interest in her verdict on performances. She asked if her ignorance gratified him. He laughed and did not disagree; restraint held him in limits, undemonstrative, apart from the plain enough deference to things she said. She might have found his lack of assertion, of edge, at times irritating; she was the sort of woman who showed appreciation regarding the blades of argument. To her husband, a man who displayed scope and patience, she said: 'I am all the time waiting, you might say I am coolly waiting, for some quickening in myself about him. My attitude towards him and me is one slightly clinical, such as I might have towards a lazily-observed experiment from which I expect, but without any great interest, some result. A few times I have said to myself: it won't happen this way; it never does. The unexpected, the unlooked-for – this is how things always happen with me.'

Derek Owens took this with his peculiar brand of equanimity. He was a man, one might have said, of existential outlook. 'It is,' he remarked with nice distance, 'a good idea never to involve the affections unless one means to be reciprocal.'

In the main Mrs Owens treated Donegan with a species of raillery, a light approach that could be taken as meant equally only to glance off the surface, or as a challenge to anchor in steadier depth. Donegan usually appeared to take the quipping in very good part, pleased at any elicitation from her, but sometimes he left abruptly, face closed. She had hurt him. If she gave any thought to such sustaining of hurt she might have been almost glad of it; possibly she might have got a degree of satisfaction in achieving a change in the too-quiescent front. But he kept forces like anger confined from her, holding himself back, very likely afraid to fill in whatever picture she might have of him.

It did not seem probable that his was a case of floating energy, requiring some object for its focusing. A great deal of his time went to his work, he was making strides, it looked as if he would be very successful. Many girls would welcome so promising a specimen but on the subject of girls he had latterly made an angular statement to Mrs Owens: 'Since you have granted the favour of some just – even – conversational outings, I have not been dating people regularly.'

'A mistake,' she said, 'I can be no answer to you.' She seemed however to believe him; he was not the lying sort. The coolness of this counsel to his single-mindedness was a register of her condition regarding him. Later she said to Derek Owens, 'I am watching for any trace of jealousy in myself.'

'Yes,' he said, 'jealousy is a clear indication of a certain kind of love.' He followed this up by adding consideringly: 'Of all sorts of love. We merely learn more about handling it with the finer sorts.'

'Finer? How jealous of him are you?'

'All must agree he and I seem very civilized to one another. I must be handling it nicely.'

'Why,' Mrs Owens spoke to her husband as to a person who handled things nicely. Wisely. 'Why, give me one good reason why I should bother with Jim Donegan? Life is so full for me it is undesirable, foolish, a vanity, to stretch it to include him. I have gone this far with him – this very acceptable distance – only because I would have been taking time off anyway to go to films, concerts, with someone, anyone. Why not sometimes with him? It has been relaxing. But to go any further, to try to move from imagination – inevitably one imagines – into action, would be unnatural. A mechanical process, the kind of thing a bored woman might do for some perverse titillation. I am never bored.'

141

To all of which Derek Owens replied levelly, 'Yes.' He added, 'It is a good idea not to evoke deliberately affections one does not mean to answer.'

Jim Donegan continued to call at the house of the Owens. He joined the family occasionally at meal-time, pot-luck haphazard meals on to which he happened. This was what he had done over the few years since knowing them, dropped in. The casualness of his calls might indeed often have annoyed Mrs Owens. She would offer him no food nor drink those times, behaving quite out of national tradition. She had given to understand sometimes that she considered much that went for Irish hospitality to be based on pride, on the fear of what people might think. She had not infrequently offended callers with her version of hospitality, or want of it. About this she did not care at all and often gave the view that home life should be inviolable, that she would not be compelled by expectation to present a false front, that if people called out of the blue they must take things as they found them and that might be less than welcoming sometimes where she was concerned.

Contrarily, she could be lavish with presence, her most expansive self, and food, on specifically arranged occasions. Derek Owens sometimes specifically invited Jim Donegan; he gave every evidence of liking him, said he felt for his bachelor-room condition, said in all their hearing that the fellow would one day make a name, would outshine himself. It could be said of Derek Owens that he was not a very usual kind of man. One way and another Jim Donegan seemed to have come to move in less awe of him.

The rest of the family could not be reported as exhibiting much enthusiasm over Donegan. His awkward ways did not appeal to them. Amongst themselves, when they had nothing better to do, they sometimes made fun of him, his accent, his curious gait, his idiosyncrasies. Sometimes they did it so Mrs Owens could hear. It was a well-sensitized family where subterfuges did not succeed and though these, in the human course of things, were resorted to by all, at some point or another, no one was really fooling anyone. 'The sooner we all laid everything out on the table the simpler it might be' was a remark – or one to similar effect – which periodically circulated in the pregnant air.

A few of the older ones gradually came to evince something of a more positive flow towards Donegan, as if they discovered, in their varying ways, the more personable material at the back of the pedantic noises, the gauche behaviour. However, the beautiful ones did not seem able always to resist temptation to mimicry, their natures so being cast, he being such asking quantity.

There came the day when, with what might have been particular courage, he asked Mrs Owens to a dance, a biggish affair got up by prestigious people for a charity drive. She accepted. One of the cool older ones opened the door to him and, rudely deliberate, stared at his unaccustomed appearance in dress clothes, impeccable as to black and white but a degree awry. His nose glistened and his face somehow looked especially nude and woundable. He had combed his hair forward from the crown, doubtless because Mrs Owens often said she liked men's hair that way. It could have been intended as quite a daring concession to her, this. When she had a few times chivvied him about his utter indifference to trendiness, he had said perhaps he was just as well that way, better for his job where one could only flaunt flightiness having got to the higher reaches and proven years. She had then told him that what he didn't see was that his very squareness was becoming obtrusive, that everyone in his department was quite liquid about clothes. He merely looked a little bulb-eyed confronted with the swing of her interest and left it to her. Now with his adventurous hair he was brought into the hall where Mrs Owens was waiting. Another one of the older ones standing on the stairs and, from that vantage, eyeing the mother's *décolletage* said, 'You're going out like that are you?' Mrs Owens gave the impression of a woman who would like to seem undisturbed. The one who had opened the door said, 'You don't need to go dancing. Dancing is for getting a man.'

'There are different ways of looking at most things,' Mrs Owens replied. She sounded mild but seemed however to decide against delaying departure by first offering the escort a drink. Such a procedure might occasion emphasis, might invite further thrusts against which she might not have felt proof just then. She could have been nervous about someone bringing up the fact of his youth, an obvious enough sharp point. She might have had her own thoughts on the disparity between illusion and reality for she once said to her husband, 'To look young is possible all right; to act young, when one is not, is perhaps sad. One should wear one's years with a clear acceptance and act accordingly.' To which homily-in-effect he had given a shade perhaps too-ready agreement. Everything considered, Deborah Owens might not have been especially comfortable about going to a dance with Jim Donegan.

She flung a general goodbye, not entirely successfully insouciant, up around the house with its registering presences, and allowed Donegan, stiff and shiningly determined, to usher her out.

Over supper he sipped wine minimally. When she went to a second cigarette straight after the first she said, 'You hate to see me smoke, don't you?'

'I like everything you do.'

'That's pathetic. Really Jim! Can't you do any better?'

'It's true. I was only thinking you would be better off every way doing something else with your mouth.'

'There is no future in this Jim for you. There is just everything against it. You are looking for a lot, investing me with all sorts of imagined qualities which I haven't, investing me with what you want to find in me. The fact that I am older signifies something in all this – that you are sort of compulsive – obsessive – about me. Maybe not healthy.'

'Men fall in love with older women all the time.'

'Maybe to regret it if the women are fools enough to take the manifestation at its face value. I don't. I suspect all this putting on a pedestal. Pure fantasy. I'm a flawed specimen, you've seen me often enough in the home setting to know; there's something disproportionate about persisting in boosting me up. I don't like it. Too unreal. Lasting things between men and women come out of a mixture of all sorts.'

'I've not had opportunity for much mixture, have I? You

see I'd like a chance for that, and I'm not put off. I find you answer a lot for me, flaws or no.'

'You imagine I do. I'm bitchy.'

'Yes, probably. So what? Derek should know it if anyone and he's not put off. You are other things also.'

'He has been, pretty nearly, time to time.' Clearly she was finding pleasure, perhaps that of perverse display, in the persisted detraction of herself. He continued, obstinate.

'I can wait.' It sounded as if he had before him a pristine virgin with a demon father.

'For what? There's no future whatever for you in me. You should be starting progeny with some young girl.'

'Maybe I might do that too, although it seems unlikely, and if I did she'd have to be the sort to accept all about you too.'

'Tall order, but an advance on Huxley.'

'There's Derek – that sort of decency . . . I despise the traditional affair.'

'And you would of course be very willing to accept her other man – men – until a natural death you did part?'

'Theoretically – yes.' He was amused. 'A lot would depend on the motives on all sides.'

'Ah well, we'll see. You can't believe you are going to continue – feeling about me? It's some kink you'll outgrow.'

'In five years I haven't outgrown it. *It* has grown.'

The weeks went on and Mrs Owens, not having a heart of stone, showed signs of being affected by him. It might be that, in full knowledge of what she was about, she began deliberately to bestow affection on him. She said one day to him, 'I am making an act of will regarding you.' It could be understood as a pretentious and conceited remark but it was said without an air. To her husband she said, 'I am astonished at the steadfastness of his waiting,' a pronouncement which could be punctured as windily romantic. Derek Owens did not treat it so. 'It is weeks after the dance and I have not even kissed him. A few times a hand on his knee, driving.'

Her husband said, 'Be careful.'

'A hand on a knee is truly portentous. Something to be very careful about.'

'All right, but you can't play about with people.'

'I am not playing.' Nor did she appear to be now. One thing that held her guarded might have been a fear of losing poise. She was thought of as relatively balanced, the years' labours having contributed to such a notion; what Jim Donegan hoped for, he might receive as a sign of deplorable imbalance; pride resisted that one should so reduce oneself before this younger man. The family, Derek excepted, would surely not spare her. They would know of course, nothing ever really being secret in their house of perspicuity. The clever ones call it senile degeneration; she might have imagined them, their bright deadly young voices. Would the carnage of their precision weapons be worthwhile when in truth she valued them all more than she could ever value someone like Jim Donegan?

She did not give the appearance of playing. She had become graver with him before the perceptive offspring. Where previously her banter had an easy spring, it now had a measured quality as if she might not wish to sound juvenile. She was possibly resolved to be her age, convey a statement of her quantum of dignity come what might after that. She grew the tint from her hair, allowing the grey its place.

A few times he took her out for a meal when her husband worked in the evenings. She would first ring Derek, telling him. These dinners were of a modest character and they had one together the night before Derek's birthday. Towards the end of the meal Jim Donegan asked with sudden urgency:

'What would you say now is the nature of our peculiar relationship?'

She considered quite a time before she said seriously, 'I would say it is in the nature of a search; for me that is. It has become that, yes.'

'So I searched him, Derek, and was not unrewarded. I feel a good deal humbler now.'

Derek Owens, man of proven resource, did not discourage her findings. He saved exclamation for Vatican proceedings when on the morning of his birthday, having fetched in the paper, he got back into bed. 'The extraordinary dogs!' He shook the daily to straighten out the creases where it had jammed in the letterbox. His wife, awake, made the expected question 'Now what?'

'They've been demoting saints. What does that footling Vatican think it's doing?'

'What's a saint? Saint my bottom.'

'Deborah, women in this holy country do not say things like that.' He sounded pleased by the coarseness. She replied with a *non sequitur*:

'How gorgeous to be able to stay here all morning.'

'Yes, gorgeous.' He agreed, interrupting his perusal of Vatican proceedings. 'Someone to do breakfast and lunch. Ours here on a tray. Heaven.'

'The person that would do that for me would be a saint,' Deborah Owens said. 'I'm a saint, you're a saint – we slog away at the daily muddle. Saints of the muddle.'

'They've pushed up Thomas More – it's a shame playing around with Saint George like that . . .' He seemed to be really feeling it; he jiggled his feet under the bedclothes and banged the cover with his hand.

'How can you get so worked up over it? Saint George wasn't even a Catholic, he wasn't even English . . .'

'Get your facts right.'

'Not sufficiently interested in those sorts of facts. I'm more interested in the facts of shopping for your honourable birthday dinner tonight – happy birthday! – and that you continue to be special and particular. O bliss!'

He put down the paper and soon it rustled to the floor. It would appear he had sure knowledge of his wife.

ROSE GREEN GOING EAST

by Adrian Kenny

The sun had been blocked by a range of snowy mountains when Rose went to wash. Now it was up. She stood in the corridor looking out of the window, her face still covered with long drops of water; in her rush she had forgotten a towel. A cold morning breeze swept along the corridor, drying and freezing her pink skin. She pulled the cord of her dressing-gown tighter around her waist – still a fine waist – and whistled three bars of a song.

The clatter of pistons came faster (da-dada-dada!) and the train rocked forward down an incline. Her plump stomach sang just as it did when her aeroplane was at last bounding off the ground or the ship's screw began to roar. The rocks outside changed gradually to sand. Acre after acre flew by – it was like another train – in an unbroken streak of brown. Suddenly the train swung to the right, facing east again. The sun shot out of sight and she was thrown back against a carriage door.

'Good morning,' cried Mustapha. He pressed a golden hand on her shoulder, quite needlessly steadying her. As usual his teeth were showing in a great smile. He cocked his head without embarrassment to gaze at Miss Green.

'Good morning,' she said. For some reason she was pretty. Her pink skin was lined. Her blonde hair was

149

riddled with darker streaks. Her large bosom still seemed to force out of her clothes but it was surely getting limp with time. She was thirty-nine.

'Good morning, Rose.' He took the hand from her shoulder and held it out. She took it, shook it.

'Ah, oh good morning!' He had a few other apt English words until Good Evening came. He grinned happily.

She lifted her eyes from the whirring landscape and half turned. He was still staring, both coppery eyes fixed without a blink. He was perhaps the same age as herself or a little younger. There was something martial about his shoulders; he looked rich; obviously he was Persian. But he was secretive in a childish way and refused to tell anyone in the carriage where he was coming from, going to. His high cheekbones and fine hooked nose made her bite down for some reason upon her own tongue.

'Very beautiful. Yes. Good morning.' He swung his hand in a gesture at the sand and sky, then laid the same hand along her shoulder. One finger fluttered along the nape of her neck. He made happy gargling sounds.

'The lavatory, Mustapha.' She pointed. 'Hurry, while it's free.' She mimed the washing of eyes and brushing of teeth. He drew tight his own, rather effeminate dressing-gown of yellow silk and padded down the swaying corridor.

Again they began to climb and the train began to veer north. The country grew rougher and stonier. The sun flashed from sight as they entered deep cuts and burst on them once more the moment they emerged. Rose folded her arms on her stomach, then raised them, raised her breasts and drew in the warming air. Hillocks, littered with brown boulders and small prickly shrubs, rolled before her over the horizon. Twice she spotted morning smoke from tiny villages: the houses were of dark mud, totally invisible to her eyes. Small boys herded goats and ran wildly to hold them back together as the noisy train approached. The sun grew warmer. She looked at her watch: it showed seven o'clock. At home now it would be four, with four hours of black night left before gloomy November dawn; she would be fast asleep in her narrow flat, perhaps turning and entering another phase of the cracked dream or nightmare.

'You're mad,' her boss, Professor Ross, had cried. 'You can't leave!'

She was not really shy but the walls of every room in the History Faculty were thin. She had slipped a fresh foolscap sheet into her typewriter as the professor began to beat the desk and whine. 'After eight years! In the middle of everything. You can't just walk out, Miss Green! Rose!'

But the rattle of the electric keys had drowned every word he said.

'Good. Good. Good,' said Mustapha. 'Yes. Yes.' He was enveloped with the scent of Muske Lavande and it swirled about the carriage as he entered. The other travellers, the Cobbs, looked up. He had combed his black hair; his face shone like brass. The train was howling as it slowed before some country station. The station master stood to attention and saluted as the train jerked to a halt. Hordes of boys leapt aboard with boxes of steaming food for sale.

'Breakfast. Please. Oh yes.' Mustapha leaned out the window and began to shout in Turkish or Persian.

Mrs Cobb was up and dressed. Her husband, Reggie, was still on the bottom bunk, gazing out the window at the sun; he was whistling *The Road to Mandalay*. His bald head swung back and forth as the train pulled out, picked up speed. Each time Rose looked at him he appeared happier.

'Five more days and we'll be in India.'

'Get up, darling,' said his wife.

'Good morning, Reggie.' Mustapha spoke thickly through a mouthful of hot peppers.

'Good morning!' Mr Cobb raised himself on one elbow. 'Good morning, Miss Green.'

He had a broad Scotch accent.

'Rose. Please.'

'Oh, Rose!' He grinned and rolled his bald head back on to the pillow and began to whistle.

His wife rubbed at his pate and then snatched away the pillow. 'Up. Up.'

'Ah, Letty.'

'Up!'

'Look away, ladies!' For such an old man he was active. 'No pyjamas.' He threw back the grey blanket and sprang

151

onto the floor. His striped underpants hung to his bony knees. Letty and Rose turned to look out the window and laughed. Again there was sand before them and the sun and now a line of swan-necked camels. As Rose looked and laughed and felt the sun strike her the train bounded up another slope, shuddering. Reggie began to sing again. They turned about.

'My Lord, I love trains!' He switched on a little electric razor and looked into the glass.

'Go down and wash properly, dear. The lavatory.'

'Engaged,' Mustapha intoned.

Rose sat by the window and leaned her head against the glass. Through the mirror Reggie looked at her. 'You won't believe me. I can't believe it. A week ago we were in Edinburgh.'

'Five days ago I left Dublin,' Rose said loudly.

'Five days and we'll be in India.' He switched off the razor and rubbed his round chin. He turned about. Rose nodded and then smiled.

Letty pulled out the table which hung beneath the window and laid out blue delph mugs and a food basket, Reggie lit the little primus stove and filled their kettle with water from a plastic bottle. Together they rubbed their hands and awaited tea.

'You won't believe me,' he said. 'I can't believe it. I haven't been out of Britain for thirty years.'

'Nor I,' said Letty. She looked invitingly at Rose. 'But I bet you have, you have the wandering look!'

Rose shook her head.

'He's a doctor,' said Letty then. 'Tied to his job.'

'Was.' Reggie measured two spoons of Lyons Green Label into the pot and poured on the boiling water. 'Retired now. Letty here did most of the work anyhow. She was a nurse.' He laughed noisily.

'Really? So was I once.'

'Once! Once? You're not retired?' And Letty laughed.

'Nurse . . .' Mustapha laid down his kebab and leaned forward. 'Nur . . . se . . .'

But Reggie apparently felt he was now in the middle of some story. As he buttered neat slices of bread and handed them on the blade of the knife to Letty, Rose and Mustapha, he plunged back into the darkest centre of his tale.

'So I was sent out to India.'

'I was born in India, you see.' Letty began to laugh. 'My father was in the army. It's that long ago.'

'I didn't know her then. But listen . . .'

'We had this water wheel at the end of the garden . . .'

'Letty, Letty.'

They both leaned forward, brimming. Rose always had this effect upon strangers. Her eyes were like deep dry bowls waiting to be filled.

'Let me, Letty.'

Letty laughed again.

Reggie leaned even further, pretending to tap at Rose's knee where it peeped out from her gown. 'You know the sort of thing. They have them in very dry land. A central water system controls the village; then on certain days the sluice-gate is opened, the water races down culverts past people's gardens . . .'

'We had a high wall around our garden.'

'Dry mud . . .'

'Very high,' said Letty.

'Ah, Letty . . .'

'But fixed into it we had this water wheel; it was driven by an old bicycle, you know what I mean. Well, this day I was all alone in the house. My parents were away in the next village. I was just eighteen then, fresh back from school. They were letting the water run and our boy was paddling away, bucketing it into our garden – oh it was parched. Then next thing he fell! It was only six or seven feet but he hit his head and just lay on the ground in the middle of the water. I ran down the path screaming of course . . .'

Reggie thrust his head – photo-finish fashion – past hers. Rose gazed from one to the other.

'I was walking down the road, the other side of the wall, you see, when I heard the commotion. I had arrived only the week before and of course I knew nothing. Later I discovered that everyone was always screaming and I took no notice at all.'

Letty hugged him. 'Over the wall he jumped. There was I up to the ends of my frock in the flood, staring at our poor boy . . .'

'And that's the way we met!'

'More?' said Letty. She held up the teapot.

'Please,' said Rose.

As Reggie passed milk and sugar he began to whistle again. Letty made a great shrug and smile. 'It's going to be the holiday of a lifetime.'

'A pilgrimage,' Reggie said. 'To all our old shrines!'

She stood out in the corridor by a half-open window when she had dressed, gazing blankly. It was beautifully warm. The train was now so fast and the land so utterly bare one could not say for sure in which direction they were going. There wasn't a living thing in sight. She looked up and down the corridor, then leaned diagonally like a sweeping-brush, head to the carriage door, feet stretched out against the other side. As the train rocked, the sun glanced like a swinging lamp on or off her body. Rose had a habit of fixing her odd eyes – they were almost green – at a focus of three or four feet, as if staring at a suspended mote of dust. She had other habits too, almost as bad, and they had all seemed to get her into trouble. She didn't seem concerned as she slowly drew down her long lashes and let the sun fill her eyelids with a liquid scarlet.

It was soon after leaving the Civil Service – in her days as a children's nurse – that she had sat one sunny autumn morning listening for fifteen minutes (ear cocked sideways with the rapt attention of a composer) to the baby's squall. The row with the mistress later had been too much for her; she had retired to her bedroom with many cigarettes and the Cork Dry Gin. 'Rose, Rose,' the Reverend Mother had said, 'I don't like the way you're going': that was the time of her first bit of trouble, and she was only sixteen. The entire school had sat down as usual in the refectory, eight o'clock, for breakfast. It was June and the sun was already hot; but no rays could enter those awkward windows. Rose had been stooped over her porridge when a sudden heat in her hair made her glance up; then the knitting-needle sun shaft had

154

caught her in the face. She had laughed very loudly and then almost screamed. A red-billed prefect tossed her into the corridor. Soon after she was expelled for rudeness. She left the next school when her father died. 'I don't know,' Mrs Green used to say, 'you certainly don't take after me.' Between her many jobs Rose lived at her mother's home, but never unpacking her cases completely. Mrs Green watched her grow fat by the eternal kitchen fire and suspected that her dozes and odd staring habits were just tricks to avoid conversation. But she took no chances and kept the gin under lock and key.

'Open,' said Mustapha. 'Very excellent.'

Rose felt the tiniest filament of frost in the air. He had opened the window fully and thrust his head out. 'Excellent. Beautiful.' The wind caught his raven hair and lifted it into a plume. He jerked back and then together they stood against the wood panelling. He had put on a loud knee-length coat of suede and green check cloth. Despite it, the scent of Muske Lavande ebbed from him.

'Please,' he then said slowly. From behind his back he produced a small book. 'What is?' He pointed out an English word XYLOPHONE a little nervously as if expecting a double meaning. The train plunged under a tunnel.

'Come back into the carriage. I'll explain.' She took him by the elbow and slid back the door; but the lights had not come on. They stood swaying in the dark till a whistle sounded and they saw then sunlight rushing in the tunnel mouth. The Cobbs were lost in a game of Scrabble. Half of the board was covered with little words: CAP – PIPE – EARTH. Reggie whistled without a pause, occasionally looking out the window as if expecting to see India pop over the next range of hills. Letty was wrapped in a red plaid rug, half dozing, half smiling.

'Climbing again,' he said as Rose sat down. 'Look at the way they do it. Build the tunnel up against the outside of the cliff like a lean-to. It's much simpler than all this blasting and boring.' The roar of the wheels on another viaduct echoed up under their feet.

'It's terrifying!' But Rose was laughing too.

When XYLOPHONE had been explained Mustapha

turned the page, running his thumb alongside each word, pronouncing it to himself, breathing deeply through his hooked nose. At last he pointed out VETERINARY SURGEON and then raised his head. He beamed as Rose explained – or tried to – and grinned all the more when she gave up. She took the book from him and rifled through it. On the right hand column were short Persian phrases and words; the English was in very black smudged print alongside. Rose saw him move closer and soon the little book rested on his left, her right, knee. His fingers were long; each joint was carefully waisted and dusted on top with barbs of fine black hair. Carefully he pointed out new words and drew his fingertip to the left hand side of the page for the English meaning. It grew into a conversation or game.

'Excuse me, where are you going to?' said the black smudgy print. She drew her finger left, to the Persian, then looked at him. Mustapha bent down to the words and then smiled furtively, pressing his hands palm to palm together. She pointed to the next question: 'Are you a tourist?' but he simply turned the page and proffered a new sentence: 'Do you like our wonderful scenery?'

The Cobbs bent a little lower over their Scrabble; the light was already getting weak. The train went faster all the time. There had been a long delay during the night which the driver seemed anxious to make up for.

'More mountains ahead,' said Reggie. As he began to speak the train flew into the tunnel. 'That's the fifth this afternoon,' he said. 'They number them in whitewash. Look back when we get out and I bet you'll see a 5.'

'You're terribly observant,' she said brightly.

Reggie bit a lip, shook his head and smiled modestly.

Mustapha nudged with his knee. 'You are pretty,' read the English of his latest phrase. He peeped sideways, raised thick eyebrows. She smiled and flicked the page. They plunged into darkness and all four sat in silence, listening to the hammering wheels below.

'I think we'll give up this game, darling,' said Letty. 'It's becoming impossible'.

'Oh Lord, I love trains,' said Reggie. They shot out into

the afternoon light; they were in a gorge with green stone rising up on either side into crags.

'Very beautiful,' said Mustapha's phrase-book. 'Who is your tailor?' Rose turned and laughed. Then she pointed to the foot of the page. 'The evenings are getting very short.'

He nodded seriously but did not seem too impressed. He bent his head and searched through the next chapter. There it was, sure enough, in two parts:

'Where is the manager? Show us to our bedroom.'

Rose's mind jumped. Up now before her eyes flashed a brilliant picture of her bed, carried from flat to bedsitter to home to flat over the last twenty years – dismantled now into two metal bars and two pitchpine endboards, lying against the whitewashed wall of her mother's cellar. She blinked then and Mustapha laughed loudly or triumphantly and all his teeth shone: the very tips of his canines had been capped with gold. He reached up to the rack for his wash-bag and from it took a bottle. Then taking Rose's fingertips he sprinkled her open palm with a few drops of something brown, like iodine. She recognized the sweet rich smell of his perfume. He folded the fingers back onto the drops, opened them and lifted them to her cheeks and to the back of her neck. 'Oh excellent. Beautiful.'

Reggie and Letty looked up, stared a half-moment together into her saucer eyes and returned to Scrabble. The train shot down another tunnel.

'Oh, it's a long one,' Rose said chattily. No one replied. First, Mustapha laid a hand on her knee and another on her neck; then she felt him coming closer. Some thought or sensation ran through her for a minute. When, inevitably, in the past, she left or was left by her few lovers she seemed to lose everything: she seemed to forget their faces, voices, even their names; yet tiny traces remained. Surely; for she felt something familiar flash by just as the Muske Lavande enveloped her. He moved nearer, nearer in the dark till a last tiny jolt of the wheels seemed to knock them mouth to mouth together. The wheels whammed louder or seemed to as he squeezed. He crushed and crumpled her till she thought she would certainly faint, but didn't and didn't care; she clung up to him and shook, watching the corner of her eye for the first light in the tunnel's end.

The sun was down in the west, behind the guard's van, when they finally descended to the plain. Rose stood in the corridor watching the darkness before her or glancing back at the final pieces of light. She was still shaking a little and raised her right hand to her nostrils every odd minute to sniff the curious perfume. Her mind was jumping like a finch, rising and falling on a thousand odd branches. She looked down at her tatty travelling clothes, thought of her fine legs under the cord trousers. All her best things were packed in one almighty suitcase: she had packed just one week before and it had taken up a full day, what with sobs and stares and turns at her mother's gin – the wardrobe key unlocked the cupboard too. Beneath the nightgowns and the boxes of Sweet Afton cigarettes were the contraceptives (both sexes provided for), a .25 pistol, King James Bible and her savings in Thos. Cook cheques.

The floor shuddered beneath her feet and she slid forward against the glass. The train brakes screeched and in the dusk she saw a village station. It had a loop siding, otherwise it seemed quite unimportant. There they waited till another train coming from the east steamed past, spouting up soot and sparks. She tried to read the village name, painted on a huge board, but it seemed unpronounceable; besides, the light was failing. It slipped slowly behind as the train pulled out. Two half-naked boys, cycling under-bar two gaunt bikes, passed them on the cinder track beyond the sleepers. A few feet further back, but still not ten feet from the line, was a terrace of red-tiled cabins. A thin girl with a red clay jar on her shoulder entered one of them, scattering a clutch of goslings before her. Rose leaned a little farther out the window and let her hair spin in the breeze. As she did a face appeared in the next cottage windows. She saw it only for a couple of seconds as the engine rolled on to the main track, beginning to pick up speed. It was framed by the faintest flicker of light, coming perhaps from an open fire. She noticed that it was pressed forwards as far as was possible, almost touching a postage stamp window pane. It was difficult to say if it was a boy or a girl, Rose just saw two soft open lips and wide shining eyes. For an entire second the eyes rested on her own. The pistons jerked more easily then and the long train pulled down the track.

She let the wind play with her a little longer, then she withdrew and jerked the window shut. After a few more minutes she went down the corridor to the washroom.

BROTHERLY LOVE

by Gillman Noonan

When Dave phoned from Clonakilty, where he was travelling for his firm, to say he had met a 'marvellous girl' and was contemplating marriage, I was sceptical, to say the least. In my experience of the brother's courtships there had been so many marvellous girls who for various reasons had turned out to be disappointments. *Two* had even decided to become nuns after walking out with him for a while. That had been a particularly trying time – though a practising Catholic himself, Dave had become neurotically convinced he was the kind of man who drove women to vows of chastity. One man reassuring another of his virility without recourse to practical demonstration proved a formidable task, so this time I was reluctant to become involved – particularly in the kind of brotherly 'vetting' he had inveigled me into on previous occasions. He seemed to think that I – a widower of fifty and fifteen years his senior – was an all-time sage in the matter of assessing the wifely qualities of young women. It was above all, I think, the happiness of my marriage that had impressed him. Having selected the best of all women for myself, there was no reason why I shouldn't help him do the same. It was useless my arguing that 'vetting' did not help much, that happiness with a woman in this life is usually in the fall of the dice.

'You must come down and meet her,' he pleaded on the phone.

'I'm working,' I said.

'You can work down here. I'll get you a nice quiet room where you can write all day if you wish. I just want you to have a look at her.'

The crudity of the expression made me shudder. Did he think I was something of a male chauvinist jobber who in the best tradition of the Irish street fair could cast an eye on a woman's haunch and say: 'There's breeding in that one all right, brother, take her'?

'Please,' he went on, 'just this last time.'

I relented. Having completed the first draft of some children's stories, I felt in need of a break. The clean surf of Inchadonny strand beckoned – but it would be the last time, I resolved. The next morning I locked my cottage, drove into Dublin to visit my son and daughter who are both married with young children, and then headed south. The weather brightened on the way, and when I stopped in front of the hotel in Clonakilty the late afternoon sun had a steady continental heat that augured well. The brother must have been on the look-out in the bar for he appeared at once.

'Hi, Tom,' he called in a very American kind of way. 'Have a nice trip?'

He looked fatter and balder than when I had last seen him, perhaps because he had shaved off his moustache. His rather big lips seemed to protrude farther than ever, giving him the expression of an eager duck.

'What's all this about marriage?' I said, leaning against the car and going straight into battle.

'No lark,' he said seriously. 'This is for real. You'll like her. Come on, she's in the lounge, her name is Twinkle.'

Twinkle turned out to be diminutive and young – scarcely out of her teens, I imagined – with long blonde hair and large eyes, one of which was slightly out of focus giving her a concussed look as if she had just fallen off a horse. I liked the look of her.

'Hi,' she smiled, thus explaining all the hi-ing.

'Twinkle's mother was Irish, a Slattery from near Clon.'

162

The fool was warming to her pedigree even before I was seated.

'A drink,' I ordered. 'A large Irish with a drop of water.'

Dave went up to the bar and I could see him watching us in the mirror. It was a familiar situation and I swore I was not going to make any hasty pronouncements. Even if I grew to dislike the girl, I was going to be guarded in my comments. I was not, after all, his marriage broker. Like or dislike hardly entered my head as I listened to Twinkle recount details of her travels from Idaho where she had lived with an uncle until he died. She seemed no different from any of the young Americans I had met who, while in Ireland, wanted to trace some Irish forebear, fitting together the jigsaw of identity that in conversation seemed of such casual interest to them but was always, one sensed, much more than that.

'How long have you known each other?' I asked her.

'About three weeks,' she said. 'I was in difficulties.'

'Oh?'

'In the sea. Dave saved my life.'

'Heavens.'

She expelled smoke. 'Yes, crazy, isn't it?'

Here we had all the ingredients of a romance à la Dave. 'There must be a happening of some kind in love, don't you agree?' he had once remarked to me. How could I tell him that in marriage the happenings were usually of a different kind? In an old-boyish way he was still madly in love with love. The older he got and the closer he seemed to epitomize the cliché figure of the sales rep, the more obsessed he became with the idea of a lasting and truly romantic relationship. It was a need with which I truly sympathized. The four years I had been a widower had weighed on me. I knew loneliness and loss, but from the brother's point of view I had at least found happiness before losing it again. To his mind it was infinitely worse never to have found it. I, moreover, would be taken seriously by a woman if I asked her to marry me. *He* had to get around the 'randy rep' image first, and even then the girl often refused to believe he didn't have a wife tucked away somewhere and was only chatting her up. Dave, I realized now listening to

him paint the future, had sold Twinkle a fairy tale and she
was believing it.

'I've had my eye on a little cottage near the strand for a
long time,' he said. 'It will be ideal for us. I'll get McGregor
to base me here permanently so I'll never be far afield and
Twinkle won't become a grass widow like the wives of most
travellers.' He squeezed her hand reassuringly and she
smiled at him.

'Won't you be lonely down there?' I ventured to her. 'It's
miles from the town.'

'Oh, no,' she smiled. 'I love isolation.'

'Twinkle paints,' the brother interjected with a gleam in
his eye as if to say: That's a quare one for you, Mr Writer.
Dave knew as much about painting as I knew about Idaho.

'Only water-colours,' said Twinkle.

'You must show me some of your work,' I smiled lamely.

'Oh, she will, she will,' said Dave. 'I'll be away for most
of the day so you'll have plenty of time to get to know each
other.'

We did have a lot of time together in the days to follow.
After breakfast Dave went off on his rounds and Twinkle
and I drove down to the beach in my battered old VW. In
the evenings we had dinner together, after which we either
all went for a walk or to the pictures, rounding off the day
with a few drinks. At first Twinkle and I were very formal
with each other. I set up my small folding table in a quiet
spot and concentrated on polishing my stories, she went off
with her books and brushes to her own favourite nook. We
had a hamper lunch and she prepared it, making very
straight comments on the kind of things she liked and
asking me about my preferences.

'Do you like pizza?' she would ask.

'I love pizza.'

'A pity you can't get it here, isn't it?'

'It sure is.'

Lapsing so easily into her style of conversation, I was
tempted to follow up with paternal riders to the effect that
as the years went by she would find there was so much else
it was a pity she could not get in this lonely corner of the
south, but I checked myself. Why shouldn't they have their

idyll for as long as it lasted? To waggle the didactic finger at other people's happiness was, anyway, the height of casuistic arrogance.

Later, Twinkle showed me her paintings – animal-like abstractions of the landscape that to my untutored eye were not at all bad – and from then on conversation became more natural between us. In a halting, preoccupied way she spoke of her family and I pieced together a childhood that must have been very unhappy, with a father in and out of a mental home and a mother who carried on with men in his absence. Eventually the mother took to drink and died of it while Twinkle was still in her mid-teens. The father being then permanently detained in the home, she was packed off to a bachelor uncle who didn't seem to care what she did once she kept out of his way.

It was a sad but typical enough story that, for me, was all the more unreal since I had no true conception of the place out of which it had been so carelessly etched. But whatever tangle of love and inherited guilt had sent her across the Atlantic, it was clear that Twinkle was now a girl with a mission, and this was the dimension that concerned me most – alarmed me indeed when in a wedding photo of her parents I noticed a marked resemblance between her father and Dave. God above! Did she really believe that Fate was offering her a rose-rimmed canvas on which all the smears of the past could be transformed, expiated even? I found this hard to believe considering her extremely dry and cryptic remarks on many things. Yet each evening when Dave sketched in a little more of the pretty scene she seemed to accept it as if he was merely corroborating what she already knew.

She was a marvellous audience for Dave's long monologues on politics and religion sublimated in his mystique of love. She hadn't a clue, of course, at least not within the heady Irish context of this brew. Once she interrupted to ask him who de Valera was. He nearly quacked into his beer. It couldn't have been worse if she had asked him who was Jesus Christ. There followed a long lecture on Dev from which I politely withdrew. When I joined them a little later he was still pouring it out and she was still lapping it up, under no apparent strain. She seemed to think that all Irishmen were thus passionately committed to the history of their country and that the sooner she started generating the same fervour the better.

She found the formula of Irish religion as embodied by Dave more puzzling since it impinged on sex and romance, two concepts the brother held strictly at arm's length when he was confident that a future bride was at the receiving end of his attentions. I was sure Dave entertained hopes of converting her but I didn't intend to be around when that campaign was launched. Indeed the situation was sufficiently trying: the nice quiet room Dave got me was separated from his own by what must have been a paper-thin wall because I went through agonies trying to drown the noises he felt obliged to make in the name of high passion suspended under the Almighty's watchful eye. The very thought of his old-young duck face necking like a sixteen-year-old in the next room was driving me batty.

Part of the trouble was that they waited for *me* to go to bed before slipping into the room – why they couldn't have done their courting in her room I failed to understand. It was really just smooching but Dave worked up enough steam to put any rutting buffalo in the shade. I could hear him heightening the tension with an ooh and a mmmmm and an umpf only to cease at some theologically crucial point with a 'No, no . . .' or a 'We mustn't . . .' gasp '. . . not yet'. Grace must flow with courtship of a bride-to-be and for Dave marrying in the blessed state of grace and romance was paramount to the restoration of the Irish language and the re-unification of the country under a government of true Republicans of his choice.

I suppose, depending on one's view of divine surveillance, this is quite in order, but to a girl of Twinkle's background it was bound to be puzzling. She was seeking terms of reference and approached the problem over lunch on the beach in a less than subtle way.

'Did you sleep with your wife before you married?' she asked between mouthfuls of lettuce-and-egg sandwich.

'No. I'd say few people had sex before marriage at that time.'

166

'Would you now?'

'Perhaps . . . perhaps not.'

The pickings were meagre there. Sucking her teeth, she probed more boldly. 'What do you do for sex?'

'Do I look as if I have to go to extraordinary lengths to get it?'

'Don't you worry about religion?' she persisted. 'It's very important in Ireland, isn't it?'

I almost laughed at the understatement. 'For some people rather too important.'

'But you do have religious . . . compunctions about sex?'

'I think at my time of life I have less a sense of sin than a sense of ugliness. That's a moral feeling too, I suppose.' I could have gone on like this for hours feeling very urbane and superior. She fell silent so I prodded a little. 'It's a question of degree. Dave, I know, is more concerned with principle than I.'

'Is there anything wrong with that?' she flew at me. 'Dave is good.'

'Unlike me?'

She pouted, plucking at the sand. My tone had already put a slight crack in the idyll. 'Dave,' she said aggressively, 'is the first man that ever took me at face value.' (He was probably afraid to ask, I thought unkindly.) 'The first man to offer me something . . . beautiful.'

'Indeed.' I felt she was acting now and disliked her for it.

'Yes, he has principles, not like most men. I respect that.' She looked up at me defiantly. 'Other men I felt I had to tell them everything about me, not Dave. It's what I am now that matters to him. He's *gen*uinely good.'

What she felt she had to tell 'other men', to whose number I now apparently belonged, came out a little later in a faintly accusing tone, as if I were partly to blame. She had been raped when she was sixteen and had had two abortions, one the following year and one when she was nineteen. I let it all come without saying a word. What was there to say? If such things were happening every day to girls from 'good' homes, why should they arouse surprise in Twinkle's unhappy, perhaps tragic, past life? She could have told Dave and it would only have sharpened the edge of his

167

zeal to save a lost soul. Indeed, *I* also firmly believed that Dave was a good man. I felt sure he would do all in his power to realize the dream. What worried me was what would happen to Twinkle when the romance of the cottage and the isolation wore off. It was probably all selfishness on my part – I didn't want an unhappy brother on my hands.

Twinkle's 'other men' view of me expressed itself that evening in an even more ardent attention to Dave's philosophizing. Eyeing me with occasional malice, she exclaimed and enthused with him, altogether creating a bizarre, up-ended picture of courtship: he the balding adolescent full of schmaltz and wet kisses, she the actress, the creature of experience and detachment turning over the passion offered her like a toy she had once played with for real. But I saw she was on edge, and that night and later her tension expressed itself in a growing reluctance for Dave's particular brand of non-sex. I was able to read undisturbed by the sighs of battle between the spirit and the flesh.

As the hours passed on the beach, however, Twinkle's hostility showed all the signs of a counter-flirtation, and I began to feel guilty at the thought that this might be what I had wanted to happen all along. From my role as clearing house for her unromantic, 'normal' self – the self she would probably have shown Dave: they had met in a crowded Dublin pub surrounded by her youthful friends – I found myself being provocatively lured as a potential lover. In some gutsy physical way I felt she wanted to humiliate me for being so aloof, perhaps debasing herself as well for playing at Romance she would have spurned in other circumstances. The complications entailed in stealing the brother's girl, however unintentionally, were simply too appalling to be considered. I decided to leave, having accomplished (or almost) what I had probably intended from the start: to break the sugary holiday-affair spell and introduce them to each other as real people. They could take it from there.

Like all weak people I wavered. Alarm at a woman's approaches is all confused with vanity to which men, I'm convinced, are even more prone than women. If the brother was balding and looked like a duck, I still had at least a fine thatch of steel-grey hair and looked no worse than a scholarly owl. Moreover, my mild flirtations since my wife's death had given me the confidence of the clinical lover – a new thing for me even at fifty. I felt I could pluck the bud and discard it with ill-effects no worse than the nostalgia of the middle-aged savant for a brighter passion. I fear I was beginning to delude myself as a kind of sophisticated degenerate.

Still, all flirtation remains safe and indulgent theory until a young girl with long blonde hair – and looking like the girls in the advertisements – runs up to you in your warm hollow in the dunes, stretches out beside you panting, squirms and mutters something about the constriction of clothes and that even on barges on the Seine now sunbathing *au naturelle* was the thing – and there and then whips off the monstrously confining chain of her tiny bra. Whatever reaction she expected of me – reprimand at which she would have scoffed or attraction which she would have rebuffed – at the time I merely remarked on the Irish weather being a fairly reliable deterrent to such exposure. But I was genuinely disturbed. Nudity is not taken to kindly in Ireland. On the beach people were passing by – sometimes appearing out of nowhere and climbing over us – and I was afraid that at any moment the local vice squad in the person of a blushing young Garda would appear and cover Twinkle's minute breasts and startlingly large nipples with his blue tunic.

Still, for all the baiting it was also a peculiarly childish act. A little later she was up and off again into the sea, complete with bra. She would have laughed at the idea, but I suspected I had become – at least for now – to some extent a father figure who would see to it that she did the right thing. What bothered me was the extent to which the father figure would do the right thing himself.

Several times I renewed my resolve to leave that evening but Twinkle – then and on the days to follow – made it increasingly difficult. She still acted as though the cottage by the sea and all that went with it were still within her grasp, but I sensed her unrest as each afternoon progressed and the hour came for her to return to the hotel and talk about it. On the point of departure she would want another dip, and then of course to dry out we would walk miles along the beach. Often she made me detour to a lovely old thatched pub at a crossroads where we drank pints of stout. She teased me, calling me her sugar daddy. Once with the locals looking sombrely at us from under their peaked caps she kissed me full on the mouth and made an erotic thing of wiping the line of froth from my upper lip with her little finger which she then licked teasingly with the tip of her tongue. She was having a great time dangling me on a string, and although I resented it I kept coming back for more.

Dave naturally noticed the change and worried, becoming more and more silent with her. When Twinkle was in the loo one evening about ten days after my arrival, I suggested that perhaps I was a gooseberry and should leave.

'No, no!' he exclaimed. 'She likes you. She told me so. It's something else.'

'Ah, dammit, maybe she wants to be alone with you again.' My sense of guilt was really working.

'No, it's something else.'

He looked up and saw Twinkle talking to a group of men at the bar, one hand resting casually on the arm of a well-dressed young man with thick black curls.

'I've seen her talking to that fellow several times,' Dave said ominously.

'Yes, he seems quite a nice bloke.'

'I know what's nice about him.' His eyes never left them. 'He's a commercial gentleman too, one of these sharp dandified blades from Dublin.'

'I think he's moving on tomorrow.'

I felt it was the last conversational lifeline I could throw before something happened, and I was right. Dave heaved himself to his feet and crossed over to the group. I rose unsteadily behind him – we had both been drinking more than was good for us. Dave quietly moved Twinkle to one side and gave the young man's patterned shirt-front a gentle shove. I knew his style. He was one of those patriotic Irishmen who would knock the bloody Brits into the sea with one clout if he got the chance, but when it came to real action he was good at shoving.

'Stay away from my girl,' he demanded.

I had the sensation that we were all going to go for our guns. The young man looked at him calmly and said: 'Who're you and who's your girl?'

'You know damn well who I am' (shove) 'and who she is' (shove).

The trouble with shoving, of course, is that it is insulting to a man's dignity, like a slap on the face. This the young man seemed to think too because his first return shove was accompanied by his fist to the region of Dave's left eye. Dave stumbled back against me and then against a barman who was passing with a bowl of soup. The two collapsed backwards in a desperate hug.

I had begun to feel sorry for my sins. A real Irish set-to was brewing, and it would surely have boiled over only that at some crucial moment in Dave's recovery Twinkle laughed. It was a nervous laugh, immediately smothered, but since she was standing with her back to the young man it was obviously directed at the brother. Dave stopped in his tracks, looked at her with profound sadness (relief too, I suspected: it would have been an unfair fight) and strode from the room, a sorry sight with his big behind spattered with vegetable soup. The young man turned to Twinkle and shrugged in apology. With a little cry she hurried out after Dave.

I went for a long walk feeling like the original Judas. By the time I returned I was fully determined to confess everything to Dave (though what I had to confess was still very vague, nothing really had happened). It was better to lose Dave's friendship than his trust. But he had locked himself into his room with a bottle of whiskey and a piece of raw beef he had sent down for and was seeing no one, not even Twinkle.

I had a large nightcap that nearly stood me on my head and climbed under the covers, but I couldn't sleep. At about three in the morning I was still trying to read when Twinkle appeared in a blue nightdress and crept in beside me. She was inclined to tremble and I put my arm around her, comforting her as best I could but saying nothing. I think we were both beginning to realize the dangers of tampering with rose-covered cottages.

We must have nodded off because the next thing I recall is the door opening and Dave in his striped pyjamas, looking woebegone and haggard, approaching the bed as if there was a time bomb in it. My involuntary start at seeing him woke Twinkle and she raised herself on one elbow, with her other arm and tangled strands of her hair thrown across my chest. We all went into a kind of freeze that could have lasted any length of time at that unreal hour, while the comedy of it flickered darkly in my mind with silly opening lines such as 'Now, Dave, it's not what you think . . .' But before I had a chance to utter any of them he retreated as spectrally as he had appeared. If he had passed out through the wall I wouldn't have been surprised.

After some more uneventful sleep I felt Twinkle leaving the bed, and I awoke fully shortly afterwards to find the sun quite warm in the room and the hands of my little clock at ten. I shaved and packed with unusual abandon, after which I called on Dave and found him making coffee with his tiny immersion heater. He was still in his pyjamas and looked like a man who was well and truly on the batter.

'Look,' I began, 'I'm leaving. About last night . . .'

'Forget it,' he said. 'It was all my fault.'

'Indeed it was,' I rounded on him. 'You've been messing about with that girl like a pious fifteen-year-old. Last night you locked your door to her, sulking. She only wanted to comfort you. Any real man would have taken her in and made love to her.'

'With this eye?' he cried.

The eye was indeed scarcely visible in its pouch of puffed and multi-hued flesh, but I still failed to make the connection with the successful performance of the love act.

'What do you think a healthy intelligent girl like Twinkle is to make of your carry-on?' I felt real anger rise in me. 'You have the typical Irish hole-and-corner approach to love. You can't even touch the body of the girl you want to marry without feeling sinful about it. A beautiful act, a beautiful creature, and you behave like a mean little fat spider weaving webs of sin around everything, debasing love to some kind of horrible exercise in degrees of passion to be discussed in whispers in the stale air of the confessional! Maybe this is how you can court an Irish girl who has been reared in the belief that her body is something dirty and evil, but for all she has gone through Twinkle certainly doesn't think that about her body – and she probably *knows* more about the wicked world at first hand than the two of us together. Do you think girls of her generation want to be treated like dolls? Oh, yes, she admired your great show of restraint but by God I think there's a limit, and when that limit has been reached a woman wants proof that she is loved as a woman and an individual and not as a soul in transit that must be kept on ice until it can start producing babies. Twinkle isn't *real* for you, she's a myth you take to adorn your own self-exalting male spiritual temple. I think you must be in love with virginity, a soft-boiled saint all runny with your own soulful importance.'

It was a great speech, the best I had ever made. I heard the universal applause of enlightened women. Dave hung his head and said nothing. His condition had probably nothing to do with priests or religion. In him had crystallized the reflexes of generations of rural Irish courtships in dark doorways and fragrant hedges where caresses had been honed by a morally brainwashed society to a fine ethic of tolerance, with ultimate union suspended like a chalice from the stars.

I was poleaxed, therefore, when he looked up at me with his one good eye and said in a voice of doom: 'All right so, we'll do it tonight.' It was his tone that made me feel I had just brutally destroyed something, an iconoclast who had shattered an altar of conceit and pomp only to realize that for some it may have had a deep and pure significance. At the back of it all, though, I suspect I was feeling a tinge of jealousy. Twinkle had been almost mine too.

'You can't,' I said tersely.

'Why not?'

'She won't let you.'

'Why won't she let me? Sure I had to hold her back.'

'She will hate you for ever for relinquishing your principles.'

'I'll let her seduce me.'

'I bet you haven't a chance.'

'Who says?' And this time he looked at me with cyclopean suspicion.

But Twinkle was nowhere to be found. Her bulky knapsack was gone, she had left without even leaving a note. At the reception desk we were told she had paid her bill in full. The main street was astir with forenoon shoppers. We stood at the door feeling like people waiting for a funeral.

'Maybe it's serious,' Dave said suddenly.

'What?'

'Maybe she'll do something foolish. I was just thinking of when I plucked her out of the sea.'

'You mean she was trying to drown herself?'

'It's possible, and now in her great loss she'll try it again.'

'What loss?' I laughed and he looked at me, hurt. In the eleventh hour we had become rivals after all.

We drove down to the beach but except for a few families it was deserted. Up and down the coast with us, but there was no sign of Twinkle. That night on our way back to Clon we pulled up at a point overlooking a small cove. In the light of the full moon we saw a couple moving along the silvered apron of the tide. For both of us Twinkle was rapidly fading into just such a romantic setting. Recalling her naked body beside me on the warm sand, I realized that Dave and I were really two of a kind in our inability ever to drink of pleasure without diluting it. I would have said so too to him and it might have made things better between us, but I sensed he was still dreaming; and anyway, I doubt if he would have understood.

THE DISTANT PAST

by William Trevor

In the town and beyond it they were regarded as harmlessly peculiar. Odd, people said, and in time this reference took on a burnish of affection.

They had always been thin, silent with one another, and similar in appearance: a brother and sister who shared a family face. It was a bony countenance, with pale blue eyes and a sharp, well-shaped nose and high cheek-bones. Their father had had it too, but unlike them their father had been an irresponsible and careless man, with red flecks in his cheeks that they didn't have at all. The Middletons of Carraveagh the family had once been known as, but now the brother and sister were just the Middletons, for Carraveagh didn't count any more, except to them.

They owned four Herefords, a number of hens, and the house itself, three miles outside the town. It was a large house, built in the reign of George II, a monument that reflected in its glory and later decay the fortunes of a family. As the brother and sister aged, its roof increasingly ceased to afford protection, rust ate at its gutters, grass thrived in two thick channels all along its avenue. Their father had mortgaged his inherited estate, so local rumour claimed, in order to keep a Catholic Dublin woman in brandy and jewels. When he died, in 1924, his two children discovered that they possessed only a dozen acres. It was locally said also that this adversity hardened their will and that because of it they came to love the remains of Carraveagh more than they could ever have loved a husband or a wife. They blamed for their ill-fortune the Catholic Dublin woman whom they'd never met and they blamed as well the new national régime, contriving in their eccentric way to relate the two. In the days of the Union Jack such women would have known their place: wasn't it all part and parcel?

Twice a week, on Fridays and Sundays, the Middletons journeyed into the town, first of all in a trap and later in a Ford Anglia car. In the shops and elsewhere they made, quite gently, no secret of their continuing loyalty to the past. They attended on Sundays St Patrick's Protestant Church, a place that matched their mood, for prayers were still said there for the King whose sovereignty their country had denied. The revolutionary régime would not last, they quietly informed the Reverend Packham: what sense was there in green-painted pillar-boxes and a language that nobody understood?

On Fridays, when they took seven or eight dozen eggs to the town, they dressed in pressed tweeds and were accompanied over the years by a series of red setters, the breed there had always been at Carraveagh. They sold the eggs in Keogh's grocery and then had a drink with Mrs Keogh in the part of her shop that was devoted to the consumption of refreshment. Mr Middleton had whiskey and his sister Tio Pepe. They enjoyed the occasion, for they liked Mrs Keogh and were liked by her in return. Afterwards they shopped, chatting to the shopkeepers about whatever news there was, and then they went to Healy's Hotel for a few more drinks before driving home.

Drink was their pleasure and it was through it that they built up, in spite of their loyalty to the past, such convivial relationships with the people of the town. Fat Driscoll, who kept the butcher's shop, used even to joke about the past when he stood with them in Healy's Hotel or stood behind his own counter cutting their slender chops or thinly slicing their liver. 'Will you ever forget it, Mr Middleton! I'd ha' run like a rabbit if you'd lifted a finger at me.' Fat Driscoll would laugh then, rocking back on his heels with a glass of stout in his hand or banging their meat on to his weighing-scales. Mr Middleton would smile. 'There was alarm in your eyes, Mr Driscoll,' Miss Middleton would murmur, smiling also at the memory of the distant occasion.

Fat Driscoll, with a farmer called Maguire and another called Breen, had stood in the hall of Carraveagh, each of them in charge of a shot-gun. The Middletons, children then, had been locked with their mother and father and an aunt into an upstairs room. Nothing else had happened: the expected British soldiers had not, after all, arrived and the men in the hall had eventually relaxed their vigil. 'A massacre they wanted,' the Middletons' father said after they'd gone. 'Damn bloody ruffians.'

The Second World War took place. Two Germans, a man and his wife called Winkelmann who ran a glove factory in the town, were suspected by the Middletons of being spies for the Third Reich. People laughed, for they knew the Winkelmanns well and could lend no credence to the Middletons' latest fantasy: typical of them, they explained to the Winkelmanns, who had been worried.

Soon after the War the Reverend Packham died and was replaced by the Reverend Hosford, a younger man who laughed also and regarded the Middletons as an anachronism. They protested when prayers were no longer said for the Royal Family in St Patrick's but the Reverend Hosford considered that their protests were as absurd as the prayers themselves had been. Why pray for the monarchy of a neighbouring island when their own island had its chosen President now? The Middletons didn't reply to that argument. In the Reverend Hosford's presence they rose to their feet when the BBC played God Save the King, and on the day of the coronation of Queen Elizabeth II they drove into the town with a small Union Jack propped up in the back window of their Ford Anglia. 'Bedad, you're a holy terror, Mr Middleton!' Fat Driscoll laughingly exclaimed, noticing the flag as he lifted a tray of pork-steaks from his display shelf. The Middletons smiled. It was a great day for the Commonwealth of Nations, they replied, a remark which further amused Fat Driscoll and which he later repeated in Phelan's public house. 'Her Britannic Majesty,' guffawed his friend Mr Breen.

Situated in a valley that was noted for its beauty and with convenient access to rich rivers and bogs over which game-birds flew, the town benefited from post-war tourism. Healy's Hotel changed its title and became, overnight, the New Ormonde. Shopkeepers had their shop-fronts painted and Mr Healy organized an annual Salmon Festival. Canon Kelly, who had at first commented severely on the habits of the tourists, and in particular on the summertime dress of the women, was in the end obliged to confess that the morals of his flock remained unaffected. 'God and good sense,' he proclaimed, meaning God and his own teaching. In time he even derived pride from the fact that people with other values came briefly to the town and that the values esteemed by his parishioners were in no way diminished.

The town's grocers now stocked foreign cheeses, Brie and Camembert and Port Salut, and wines were available to go with them. The plush Cocktail Room of the New Ormonde set a standard: the wife of a solicitor, a Mrs O'Brien, began to give six o'clock parties once or twice a year, obliging her husband to mix gin and Martini in glass jugs and handing round herself a selection of nuts and small Japanese crackers. Canon Kelly looked in as a rule and satisfied himself that all was above board. He rejected, though, the mixture in the jugs, retaining his taste for a glass of John Jameson.

From the windows of their convent the Loreto nuns observed the long, sleek cars with GB plates, and English and American accents drifted on the breeze to them. Mothers cleaned up their children and sent them to the Golf Club to seek employment as caddies. Sweet shops sold holiday memories. The brown, soda and currant breads of Murphy-Flood's bakery were declared to be delicious. Mr Healy doubled the number of local girls who served as waitresses in his dining-room, and in the winter of 1961 he had the builders in again, working on an extension for which the Munster and Leinster Bank had lent him £22,000.

But as the town increased its prosperity Carraveagh continued its decline. The Middletons were in their middle-sixties now and were reconciled to a life that became more uncomfortable with every passing year. Together they roved the vast lofts of their house, placing old paint tins and flower-pot saucers beneath the drips from the roof. At night they sat over their thin chops in a dining-room that had once been gracious and which in a way was gracious still, except for the faded appearance of furniture that was dry from lack of polish and of wallpaper that time had rendered colourless. In the hall their father gazed down at them, framed in ebony and gilt, in the uniform of the Irish Guards. He had conversed with Queen Victoria and even in their middle-sixties they could still hear him saying that God and Empire and Queen formed a trinity unique in any worthy soldier's heart. In the hall hung the family crest, and on ancient Irish linen the Cross of St George.

The dog that accompanied the Middletons now was called Turloch, an animal whose death they dreaded for they felt they couldn't manage the antics of another pup. Turloch, being 13, moved slowly and was blind and a little deaf. He was a reminder to them of their own advancing years and of the effort it had become to tend the Herefords and collect the weekly eggs. More and more they looked forward to Fridays, to the warm companionship of Mrs Keogh and Mr Healy's chatter in the hotel. They stayed longer now with Mrs Keogh and in the hotel, and idled longer in the shops, and drove home more slowly. Dimly, but with no less loyalty, they still recalled the distant past and were listened to without ill-feeling when they spoke of it and of Carraveagh as it had been, and of the Queen whose company their careless father had known.

The visitors who came to the town heard about the Middletons and were impressed. It was a pleasant wonder, more than one of them remarked, that old wounds could heal so completely, that the Middletons continued in their loyalty to the past and that in spite of it, they were respected in the town. When Miss Middleton had been ill with a form of pneumonia in 1958 Canon Kelly had driven out to Carraveagh twice a week with pullets and young ducks that his housekeeper had dressed. 'An upright couple,' was the Canon's public opinion of the Middletons and he had

179

been known to add that eccentric views would hurt you less than malice. 'We can disagree without guns in this town,' Mr Healy pronounced in his Cocktail Room, and his visitors usually replied that as far as they could see that was the result of living in a Christian country. That the Middletons bought their meat from a man who had once locked them into an upstairs room and had then waited to shoot soldiers in their hall was a fact that amazed the seasonal visitors. You lived and learned, they remarked to Mr Healy.

The Middletons, privately, often considered that they led a strange life. Alone in their beds at night they now and again wondered why they hadn't just sold Carraveagh forty-eight years ago when their father had died; why had the tie been so strong and why had they in perversity encouraged it? They didn't fully know, nor did they attempt to discuss the matter in any way. Instinctively they had remained at Carraveagh, instinctively feeling that it would have been cowardly to go. Yet often it seemed to them now to be no more than a game they played, this worship of the distant past. And at other times it seemed as real and as important as the remaining acres of land, and the house itself.

'Isn't that shocking?' Mr Healy said one day in 1967. 'Did you hear about that, Mr Middleton, blowing up them post offices in Belfast?'

Mr Healy, red-faced and short-haired, spoke casually in his Cocktail Lounge, making midday conversation. He had commented in much the same way at breakfast-time, looking up from the *Irish Independent*. Everyone in the town had said it too: that the blowing up of sub-post offices in Belfast was a shocking matter.

'A bad business,' Fat Driscoll remarked wrapping the Middletons' meat. 'We don't want that old stuff all over again.'

'We didn't want it in the first place,' Miss Middleton reminded him. He laughed, and she laughed, and so did her brother. Yes, it was a game, she thought; how could any of it be as real or as important as the afflictions and problems of the old butcher himself, his rheumatism and his reluctance to retire? Did her brother, she wondered, privately think so too?

'Come on, old Turloch,' he said, stroking the flank of the red setter with the point of his shoe, and she reflected that you could never tell what he was thinking. Certainly it wasn't the kind of thing you wanted to talk about.

'I've put him in a bit of mince,' Fat Driscoll said, which was something he often did these days, pretending the mince would otherwise be thrown away. There'd been a red setter about the place that night, when he waited in the hall for the soldiers: Breen and Maguire had pushed it down into a cellar, frightened of it.

'There's a heart of gold in you, Mr Driscoll,' Miss Middleton murmured, nodding and smiling at him. He was the same age as she was, 66; he should have shut up shop years ago. He would have, he'd once told them, if there'd been a son to leave the business to. As it was he'd have to sell it and when it came to the point he found it hard to make the necessary arrangements. 'Like us and Carraveagh,' she'd said, even though on the face of it it didn't seem the same at all.

Every evening they sat in the big old kitchen, hearing the news. It was only in Belfast and Derry, the wireless said; outside Belfast and Derry you wouldn't know anything was happening at all. On Fridays they listened to the talk, in Mrs Keogh's bar and in the hotel. 'Well, thank God it has nothing to do with the South,' Mr Healy said often, usually repeating the statement.

The first British soldiers landed in the North of Ireland, and soon people didn't so often say that outside Belfast and Derry you wouldn't know anything was happening. There were incidents in Fermanagh and Armagh, in Border villages and towns. One Prime Minister resigned and then another one. The troops were unpopular, the newspapers said; internment became part of the machinery of government. In the town, in St Patrick's Protestant Church and in the Church of the Holy Assumption, prayers for peace were offered, but no peace came.

'We're hit, Mr Middleton,' Mr Healy said one Friday morning. 'If there's a dozen visitors this summer it'll be God's own stroke of luck for us.'

'Luck?'

'Sure, who wants to come to a country with all that mularkey in it?'

'But it's only the North.'

'Tell that to your tourists, Mr Middleton.'

The town's prosperity ebbed. The Border was more than sixty miles away, but over that distance had spread some wisps of the fog of war. As anger rose in the town at the loss of fortunes so there rose also the kind of talk there had been in the distant past. There was talk of atrocities and counter-atrocities, and of guns and gelignite and the rights of people. There was bitterness suddenly in Mrs Keogh's bar because of the lack of trade, and in the empty hotel there was bitterness also.

On Fridays, only sometimes at first, there was a silence when the Middletons appeared. It was as though, going back nearly twenty years, people remembered the Union Jack in the window of their car and saw it now in a different light. It wasn't something to laugh at any more, nor were certain words that the Middletons had gently spoken, nor were they themselves just an old, peculiar couple Slowly the change crept about, all around them in the town, until Fat Driscoll didn't wish it to be remembered that he had ever given them mince for their dog. He had stood with a gun in the enemy's house, waiting for soldiers so that soldiers might be killed; it was better that people should remember that.

One day Canon Kelly looked the other way when he saw the Middletons' car coming and they noticed this movement of his head, although he hadn't wished them to. And on another day Mrs O'Brien, who had always been keen to talk to them in the hotel, didn't reply when they addressed her.

The Middletons naturally didn't discuss these rebuffs but they each of them privately knew that there was no conversation they could have at this time with the people of the town. The stand they had taken and kept to for so many years no longer seemed ridiculous in the town. Had they driven with a Union Jack now they would, astoundingly, have been shot.

'It will never cease.' He spoke disconsolately one night, standing by the dresser where the wireless was.

She washed the dishes they'd eaten from, and the cutlery. 'Not in our time,' she said.

'It is worse than before.'

'Yes, it is worse than before.'

They took from the walls of the hall the portrait of their father in the uniform of the Irish Guards because it seemed wrong to them that at this time it should hang there. They took down also the crest of their family and the Cross of St George, and from the vase on the drawing-room mantelpiece they removed the small Union Jack that had been there since the Coronation of Queen Elizabeth II. They did not remove these articles in fear but in mourning for the *modus vivendi* that had existed for so long between them and the people of the town. They had given their custom to a butcher who had planned to shoot down soldiers in their hall, and he in turn had given them mince for their dog. For fifty years they had experienced, after suspicion had seeped away, a tolerance that never again in the years that were left to them would they know.

One November night their dog died and he said to her after he had buried it that they must not be depressed by all that was happening. They would die themselves and the house would become a ruin because there was no one to inherit it, and the distant past would be set to rest. But she disagreed: the *modus vivendi* had been easy for them, she pointed out, because they hadn't really minded the dwindling of their fortunes while the town prospered. It had given them a life, and a kind of dignity; you could take a pride out of living in peace.

He did not say anything and then, because of the emotion that both of them felt over the death of their dog, he said in a rushing way that they could no longer at their age hope to make a living out of the remains of Carraveagh. They must sell the hens and the four Herefords, and as he spoke he watched her nodding, agreeing with the sense of it. Now and again, he thought, he would drive slowly into the town, to buy groceries and meat with the money they had saved, and to face the silence that would sourly thicken as their own two deaths came closer and death increased in another part of their island. She felt him thinking that and she knew that he was right. Because of the distant past they would die friendless. It was worse than being murdered in their beds.

CONTRIBUTORS

PATRICK BOYLE Born Ballymoney, Co. Antrim, 1905. His first book *In The Night All Cats Are Grey* placed him in the forefront of contemporary Irish short story writers and he followed with a novel *Like Any Other Man*. Was for many years manager of a Bank in the south of Ireland. Recently retired and now lives in Co. Dublin.

PATRICK BURKLEY Born Tralee, Co. Kerry, 1951. Educated at Clongowes and privately, he was for a time a clockmaker in the family firm. Won a Hennessy Literary Award in 1971.

EMMA COOKE Born Portarlington, Co. Leix, 1934. Married, she has a large family and lives in Limerick.

MICHAEL CURTIN Born Limerick, 1942, he has had a number of stories in the 'New Irish Writing' page.

ITA DALY Born Co. Leitrim, 1944, her first stories appeared in the 'New Irish Writing' page and she has also had work published in the U.S.A. A Hennessy Literary Award winner in 1972, she is a teacher, living in Dublin.

DESMOND HOGAN Born Ballinasloe, Co. Galway, 1951. 'New Irish Writing' has published many of his stories since his first one when he was seventeen, and his work has also appeared in *Transatlantic Review* and other British and Irish periodicals. He won a Hennessy Literary Award in 1971.

MAEVE KELLY Born Dundalk, 1930, she is married, with a family. Her first stories appeared in the 'New Irish Writing' page and she won a Hennessy Literary Award in 1972.

ADRIAN KENNY Born Dublin, 1945. His first stories appeared in the 'New Irish Writing' page and he was also represented in the Faber and Faber *Introduction 5* volume.

BENEDICT KIELY Born Co. Tyrone, 1919. He has published many novels and short stories and is one of Ireland's best known writers.

PETER LUKE Born 1919. Author of the celebrated play *Hadrian The Seventh*, he lived for ten years in Ireland.

JOHN McARDLE Born near Castleblayney, Co. Monaghan, 1939. A prominent Gaelic Footballer and one of the leading amateur actors in Ireland, his first stories were published in the 'New Irish Writing' page and he won a Hennessy Literary Award in 1974. A teacher, he is married and has two children.

JOHN McGAHERN Born Co. Leitrim, 1935, he has published three novels and one volume of short stories which have put him in the front rank of contemporary writers.

GILLMAN NOONAN Born Kanturk, Co. Cork, 1937. He has travelled and worked in various parts of Germany and Switzerland.

EITHNE STRONG Born West Limerick, 1923. Married, with a large family, she lives in Dublin. Since her first story was in the 'New Irish Writing' page in 1968 she has had many more stories published and has also brought out a collection of poems.

WILLIAM TREVOR Born Mitchelstown, Co. Cork, 1928. Winner of the Hawthornden Prize in 1965, his novels and stories have gained him a wide reputation on both sides of the Atlantic, and he is also the author of many distinguished plays for television.

TERENCE de VERE WHITE Born Dublin, 1912. Literary Editor of *The Irish Times*, he has published many novels and biographies, and is one of Ireland's most distinguished men of letters.